# The Next Sorcerer
by

## Joy Brighton

**The Next Sorcerer**

Cover Art by *Jennifer Greeff*

The Wild Rose Press, Inc.
PO Box 708
Adams Basin, NY 14410-0708
Visit us at www.thewildrosepress.com

Publishing History
First Edition, 2022
Trade Paperback ISBN 978-1-5092-3732-6
Digital ISBN 978-1-5092-3733-3


Published in the United States of America

I hiked the rest of the way up the Verde Canyon. The scum-coated stones in the center of the stream crunched dry and crusty under my shoes. Enormous red sandstone walls echoed my footsteps.

A lizard skittered out from under a rock and dashed for cover into a heap of fallen cottonwood leaves. I dodged sideways, giving the critter a chance to escape.

Rounding the bend of the stream, I froze and sucked in a quick breath. My stomach did a free fall off a zillion-foot cliff.

The ghost of the Magician.

The ancient shaman stood on the banks of the creek. Silent. Solid. Commanding. His arms were folded, as if he'd been waiting a very long time.

My muscles clenched, I stomped forward. I hadn't seen this troublemaker in over three years. And now here was the creep of a ghost who'd caused all my problems.

Still dressed in an ancient deerskin kilt and woven reed sandals, the ghost stared back at me, seemingly unaware of my fierce glare.

"What do you want?" I demanded, unwilling to play guessing games, especially with a stupid ghost who'd been dead for eight hundred years.

Without a sound, the Magician turned and headed upstream. He walked like any man would walk, glancing back once, as if to make sure I was following.

"No. I won't help you," I shouted.

"You-oo-oo." My words echoed in the narrow canyon.

The ghost continued down the rough trail.

"Hell." I kicked a rock and followed.

## Praise for Joy Brighton

Joy Brighton has won multiple writing contests for her works, including a first place in a Linda Howard and several placements in the prestigious Daphne Du Maurier for mystery and suspense. (unpublished)

## Dedication

For the real Ghost.

## PROLOGUE

"Freakin' weird." My whisper echoed in the otherwise silent cave. Cold sweat chilled my neck, but I took another hesitant step forward and squinted into the darkness. A fresh batch of goose bumps crept down my arms.

I wasn't alone. In a single ray of light shot from the morning sun stood the ghost who had haunted me for months.

The Magician.

The spirit waited in the back of the cave, where the jagged rock wall sloped toward the uneven floor. He'd been a tall, powerful man—a shaman. His long, black hair, threaded with silver and woven with eagle feathers, hung over massive, scarred shoulders, and a red ceremonial cloak covered one arm. The ancient ghost's strange, light brown eyes watched me, but he remained silent.

I tried to swallow, but the dust in the cave clogged my throat, and I coughed. Dragging my palms down my T-shirt, I gulped in stale air and the strangling stink of death.

"I-I brought your tools." I inched toward the shallow grave in the middle of the cave and knelt beside it. The creepy blank sockets of a human skull stared up at me, and a new rash of terror itched down my spine. I struggled to breathe past my fear.

The ghost stepped forward and pointed to the seed basket in my hand.

I nodded and placed the tiny artifact next to the skeleton's fingers.

Beside the long arm bones, white with age, the Magician's weapons had been scattered centuries before by a hasty grave robber. I rearranged the treasure of tools, spears, and amulets into a respectful order.

Wiping my damp forehead with the back of my hand, I took out the bone flute and water pot from my sweatshirt pocket and added them to the collection. It was totally weird, but somehow I knew where they belonged.

The Magician moved closer, still silent. The filtered light changed, glowing off the walls in a white-purple fusion of many colors. An echo of drums pounded from somewhere in the back of the cave. Louder. Louder. Until my ears throbbed with the beat.

I took the turquoise and silver amulet of the long-toothed cat from around my neck and placed it on the dusty bones of the skeleton's rib cage.

The Magician nodded.

I stood, brushed off my jeans, and licked my dry lips. I'd restored the last missing artifact to the shaman's grave. I waited, breathless. Something should happen.

Then the drums went silent, and the weird light began to fade. The Magician turned, took a step, and disappeared into the darkness.

"That's *it?*" I gave a disgusted snort and shook my head.

What a letdown.

"You coulda said thank you," I shouted into the

emptiness.

I stumbled toward the opening of the cave and blinked into the glare of the sun. A pair of golden eagles circled and called to each other beyond the edge of the high desert cliff.

After drawing a clean breath, I surveyed the valley floor a thousand feet below. A cool sense of relief rushed over me. My pounding heart slowed, and the buzzing fear tingling my fingers began to fade.

Finally! The Magician had his stupid sacred tools and could now rest in the next world. The strange spirit would no longer haunt me.

Feeling a warm weight on my chest, I glanced down and gasped. The cat amulet I left for the Magician now hung around my neck again. I turned back to the cave, but the entrance to the grave site had disappeared.

# CHAPTER 1

*Three years later*

"Get outta here, Josh. I'll stock the shelves." Cousin George dumped a shipping box of plastic toys onto the worn plank floor of our Trading Post. The old man turned toward me, worry lines folding his brow.

"I was trying to help," I argued, in no mood to listen to anyone, especially my grumpy old guardian. Stuffing fake arrowheads and cheap T-shirts onto a sagging wooden shelf was at least something to do on this horrible day.

George fisted his knuckles on his hips and thrust his nose forward. "I don't want you scaring off customers with your sour scowl."

"You're one to talk."

George steamed out a long sigh and ran a hand down one of his silver braids. "Okay, I know today's tough for you."

I grunted and dug my hands into my pockets, but failed to swallow the rock-sized lump stuck in my throat. Why couldn't he just let it go? Just leave me alone?

"Go for a hike," George suggested. "Tomorrow won't be so hard."

I didn't speak. Couldn't.

With a frustrated wave of his hand, George

stomped into the storeroom for another load of packing boxes.

I closed my eyes to block the sting. Fifteen and a half was too damn old to cry. "Eight more hours until tomorrow. Just get through the day," I muttered under my breath, and started loading the next shelf with bright-colored T-shirts and baseball caps.

Tomorrow would be better.

Couldn't get much worse.

The bell on the screen door of the Trading Post clanged, and a pack of teenage boys barged inside.

"Great." I muttered. "Like I needed these assholes ragging on me today." Ignoring my former friend, I stooped to pick up the box cutter and sliced through the shipping tape on the next carton.

Dennis clomped over between the glass display cabinets and planted his big black cowboy boots next to my knee.

I kept my focus on the unopened carton, but my stomach did a three-sixty with a double twist. I gritted my teeth and rose. At least I could look my former best friend in the eye these days. I'd grown five and three-quarters inches in the last four months.

"S'up, Kwail?" Dennis sneered as he drew out my name.

"What do you want, Dennis?"

Dressed in a plaid cowboy shirt and ripped-before-you-buy-them jeans, Dennis Robb tipped back the high-priced Stetson his daddy bought him and spread his legs like a tough guy. "Thirsty. We came for sodas."

"Sure."

With cold blue eyes, Dennis glared at me and then around the room. "Nothing else worth buying in this piece-a-crap store." He kicked the box of plastic toys at my feet. The boys behind him sniggered, and he flashed a toothy grin at them.

I rubbed my aching jaw and bit down on the inside of my lip. He's not worth it. Don't let him get to you.

Dennis settled his thumbs inside his belt buckle. "Nothin' but a heap o' shit."

The angry heat in my chest rose and burned into my brain. A red blur blocked my vision. I gripped the box cutter until my fingers ached with pressure.

George stepped between us and eased the cutter from my cramped hand. "You got money?" he asked the boys.

"Sure, sure. I'm buyin' today." Dennis dug in his front pocket and pulled out a wad of cash. Big bills.

"That'll do." George grabbed a twenty and pointed to the rusted case of cold sodas by the door.

I stomped across the room in the opposite direction and hung onto the back of George's old rocking chair. I stared at the rusty-black potbelly stove huddled in the corner and counted my heartbeats. Dennis was such a freakin' showoff.

A scuffle of feet. A jostle of bodies. A clink of bottles. Finally, the boys took off, laughing and shoving each other.

"Peace out, Kwail," Dennis called before he slammed the front door.

George crossed his arms over his barrel chest and huffed out a breath. "Why do you let them bully you?"

I gave the rocker a vicious shove. "Oh, right. Like I should go a couple of rounds with the sheriff's son? Real smart. Or take on that whole pack of losers?"

"Bunch of hyenas." George growled and flipped

one of his braid off his shoulders. The lines around his mouth and his black eyes deepened. He rubbed his chin thoughtfully. "Is he a bully at school?"

"Nah, no way." I stuffed my hands in my pockets.. "Least not when anyone's looking."

George rang up the sale on the old brass cash register. "Go take that hike now." His voice sounded calm, but he slammed the cash drawer so hard the glass counter shook.

"Maybe." I headed through the stockroom, out the back entrance of the Trading Post, and into the alley.

What else could go wrong on the worst day of the whole year?

# CHAPTER 2

I sprinted all the way to the creek. When I couldn't catch air after several miles, I stopped and braced my hands on my knees. My lungs burned, and sweat dripped off my chin, but I did feel better.

The October sun warmed my back. The canyon was silent. No breeze this afternoon. After the long, hot summer without rain, the riverbed was almost dry. A shallow run of green water trickled between the huge rocks.

I hiked the rest of the way up the Verde Canyon. The scum-coated stones in the center of the stream crunched dry and crusty under my shoes. Enormous red sandstone walls echoed my footsteps.

A lizard skittered out from under a rock and dashed for cover into a heap of fallen cottonwood leaves. I dodged sideways, giving the critter a chance to escape.

Rounding the bend of the stream, I froze and sucked in a quick breath. My stomach did a free fall off a zillion-foot cliff.

The ghost of the Magician.

The ancient shaman stood on the banks of the creek. Silent. Solid. Commanding. His arms were folded, as if he'd been waiting a very long time.

My muscles clenched, I stomped forward. I hadn't seen this troublemaker in over three years. And now here was the creep of a ghost who'd caused all my problems.

Still dressed in an ancient deerskin kilt and woven reed sandals, the ghost stared back at me, seemingly unaware of my fierce glare.

"What do you want?" I demanded, unwilling to play guessing games, especially with a stupid ghost who'd been dead for eight hundred years.

Without a sound, the Magician turned and headed upstream. He walked like any man would walk, glancing back once, as if to make sure I was following.

"No. I won't help you," I shouted.

"You-oo-oo." My words echoed in the narrow canyon.

The ghost continued down the rough trail.

"Hell." I kicked a rock and followed.

The Magician stopped and waited near the petroglyph of the cat. The largest drawing scratched into the blackened walls of the canyon, the cat reminded me of something out of a little kid's picture book of prehistoric animals. Long, curved teeth and sharp claws, it appeared surprisingly ferocious.

The Magician stood to one side, waiting, pointing toward the cat.

I grimaced and spit in the dust. "I won't."

The Magician's gaze never left the drawing.

"I can't see things anymore."

The echo returned to me. "Any-more, more, 'ore."

The Magician stared.

I dropped my chin to my chest and forced out a quick breath with several curses attached. Stupid ghost had more time than I ever would. Might as well get this over with. Then he'd leave me alone.

"Just this once." Reaching over my head, I touched

the wall. I traced the curve of the cat's teeth, and then closed my eyes. I let down the guard I'd so carefully built and allowed my mind to see.

The vision roared into me, smashing down my barriers like a monster truck at a demolition derby.

*The same canyon. The same man. Although he was much younger, and very much alive.*

*Dressed as a shaman, in fine, ancient robes and eagle feathers, he worked to etch a drawing into the rock. On his neck, an amulet of the cat, the sacred symbol of his clan, gleamed in the light.*

I yanked my hand away and rubbed it on my jeans until it stopped tingling. "You drew this?"

I didn't expect a response. I didn't get one.

Instead, the ghost pulled a familiar-looking bone flute from a brightly painted pouch at his waist. He walked to the river's edge and folded his legs under him. The canyon waited in breathless silence. Not even the golden leaves of the cottonwoods rustled above us. The shaman lifted the instrument to his mouth, and music flowed.

I flopped belly-down on the soft sand nearby. Anger and impatience still surged through the muscles of my back and jaw. When would he get to the point?

Wait. I tipped my head, listening more carefully, and my heartbeat grew even heavier. I remembered this melody…from somewhere.

I frowned and propped my chin on my hands. Had I heard the tune at a tribal ceremony? Or was the song hidden in my memory?

A fierce ache clutched at my chest, like the

knifelike talons of an eagle. I grimaced at the sudden, unrelenting pain. Yes. I knew the song.

I jumped to my feet. "My mom used to sing that to me."

Digging my fingernails into my palms to ease the tightness in my chest, I stared at the sky. "You don't need to remind me," I spat out the words that choked me like a hangman's noose. "I know what day it is. I remember. It's been three years. Three years ago today, my mother was murdered."

"Murdered, -urdered…-ed," the canyon echoed.

I glanced around, but the Magician had disappeared.

****

Nothing would make this miserable day go any faster. I huddled on a sandbank above the river, resting my tired shoulders on a water-smoothed boulder. I glanced up at the strip of turquoise sky visible between the narrow canyon walls and hitched in a long breath.

Like the Magician needed to remind me of past horrors. I rested my chin on my knees and curled my arms into a circle. The memories twisted my gut.

The stench of her bedroom. My mother's glazed-over eyes, staring up at me. She'd been so very still. So very dead.

It had been three years and sixteen hours since she was murdered, and I was abandoned.

I had no family now, unless I counted George, which sometimes I did, and sometimes I didn't.

I threw a sharp stone into the nearby waterfall. And what relation was George? A second cousin? A third? Someone from my father's side I hadn't even known until I was dumped at the Trading Post with the grumpy old man.

I rubbed the pain of loss gnawing under my ribs. Did I feel any different now than the day I discovered my mother's body? My fingers clamped into tight fists.

No.

Would the pain ever go away? I dropped my hands. Never.

A laugh echoed above the rushing water of the creek. A girl's laugh.

I ground my teeth. The last thing I wanted was company, especially some gaggle of tourists who'd hiked up river to gawk at the hundreds of native petroglyphs covering the canyon walls.

I scrambled back from the creek's edge, hid behind a mesquite bush, and peered out from between the branches.

The laughing girl moved into view.

I waited for more people, but she appeared to be hiking alone.

I squinted into the slanting afternoon light. From this distance, I didn't recognize her, but she had to be about my age.

Her brown hair was pulled over one shoulder. Her skin was tan against faded cutoffs and white T-shirt, but not the russet brown of a native like me.

I settled onto my haunches and watched her. She hopped effortlessly from rock to rock, making good time coming upriver, even with the day pack on her back.

Must be that new girl from California. The one with the weird name.

Forrest?

She stopped midstream, a dozen yards from me,

and I caught a glimpse of her face. Yeah. It was Forrest, all right. She'd been at the cross-country meeting last week at school.

Besides, how could I miss a girl like her? I'd seen her roaring into the school parking lot a couple times in her hideous pink jeep.

My calf muscles ached, but I didn't dare move. She'd think I was spying. The corner of my mouth twitched into a surprising smile. I was spying.

The girl jumped onto a large rock midstream and into a patch of sunlight.

I held my breath to keep from making a sound. Her hair wasn't really brown. It was a hundred shades of copper and gold, glowing in the afternoon sunlight.

She widened her stance, locked her knees, and held out her palms to the sun, as if she were a space satellite gathering energy. Her chin tilted up, and she smiled. "I'm solar powered, you know." She turned in my direction.

I couldn't swallow against my dry throat. Shit. She was staring right at me.

"I can keep going if you'd rather not talk."

I stood and walked out from behind the bush. The back of my neck itched and burned. Don't blush, idiot. Just don't blush.

She continued to watch me.

I blushed anyway, big time.

"Sorry." I struggled to find a casual tone. "I didn't want to get stuck playing native guide if you were with a bunch of tourists."

Forrest hopped off the rock, landing on the dry sand next to me. She held out her hand and met my gaze with a frankness I wasn't used to. No matter how hard I tried, the damn blush crept further up my neck.

Suddenly she dropped her hand, turned a bright pink, and lowered her eyes. "Oh, jeez, sorry, I forgot. Are you Apache? Gran keeps saying I need to be polite, not stare into people's eyes, but I'm not used to remembering your customs yet." She wiped her hand on the back of her shorts and turned to leave.

"No, wait. It's okay. I'm not Apache. I'm Yavapai and Hopi."

She stared at her tennis shoes, her knees tight together, her arms stiff and motionless at her sides. "My name's Forrest."

"Josh."

"Yeah, I know."

I studied her more closely, and her face darkened to an even deeper pink. Kinda cute. Her nose tilted up slightly on the tip. Her lips were full and smooth. Pretty. Delicate.

No. Wrong word. She had a strong face under the softness. Purposeful.

"My gran loves your dad's store," she stammered, still staring at the ground. "She dragged me in there one day. I saw your photo on the wall above the register— the one in your track uniform. You're holding a trophy."

I rolled my eyes. "Cousin."

"Huh?"

"George is my cousin, second cousin. Wish he'd take the stupid picture down. It's from freshman year."

With a grin, she swung the small daypack off her shoulders. "Want some water? I brought an extra bottle."

She sank to her knees and dug in the pack, pulling

out a plastic bag of cookies along with the bottles.

I shrugged, sat by her side and accepted the drink. "Thanks." Suddenly thirsty, I chugged half in one long gulp.

She handed me a cookie. "They're on the healthy side." With a wry grimace, she nibbled one corner of hers. "Gran has this thing about processed sugar."

"Taste good to me." I stuffed the entire oatmeal cookie into my mouth. Even before I finished chewing, I asked, "What did you mean, solar powered?"

Forrest crossed her legs under her and shrugged one thin shoulder. "I moved here last month from Northern California with my grandmother. We don't get the same kind of sunlight Arizona has. So-o, any day without fog in Pescadero was a day I would be out soaking in the rays. This light makes me feel good, like I'm energized." She lowered her eyelids and faced the sun full-on. The freckles on her upturned nose were a soft golden color in the light.

After a moment, she stared across the canyon. "Think I'm crazy?"

"Nope."

She turned back to me and grinned again. Her eyes were large, and winter's day blue, with flecks of green circling the pupil. Her lashes were dark, but clean.

I smiled back.

"I need to get going," she said as she stood. "Gran wants me home by six."

I jumped up. "I can show you a shortcut."

She giggled and brushed the sand off her butt. "Thought you didn't want to play native guide?"

"Maybe I want some more of your grandmother's cookies." I took a step toward the shortcut, ready to lead the way.

"No thanks."

"See you at school tomorrow?" The green highlights in her eyes dazzled me, and I felt a little light-headed.

She licked her lips. "Maybe."

I didn't push. If she wanted time on her own, I understood her need better than most. I gave her a quick wave and headed upstream. She turned back toward the trailhead.

I waded through the shallow part of the creek. Maybe I'd visit the old ruins today. It was only a couple of miles. George wouldn't care, as long as I got home before dark. I checked the position of the sun in the western sky. I had two hours, easy.

I jumped over a downed log and broke into a trot, feeling lighter than I had in days.

I'd only gone a hundred yards when Forrest screamed.

CHAPTER 3

Her second scream cranked my gut into a painful spasm. I reversed direction, hit the streambed, and splashed through the gaps between the boulders. Faster that way.

I stumbled on a slick log and landed on my hands and knees in a shallow pool. I tried to run, but the bottom mud tugged at my sneakers.

Another scream. Wet and bruised, I powered forward, down the far side of the creek. The agave plants sliced at my jeans and bloodied my thigh. I hissed at the pain, but had to keep moving.

There. Ahead. To the right. Her bright hair bounced color into my vision.

I scrambled over a fallen sycamore log. "Forrest," I yelled when I thought she could hear me.

She turned to stare. Her eyes were so wide, the white showed all around. Her mouth was nothing but a gaping hole. She covered her face with her hands, as if holding back another scream, and buried her face against my shoulder.

"It's okay. What?" I asked, breathing like a blown quarter horse. "What's wrong?"

Trembling, she shook her head.

I wrapped an arm around her. Then the smell hit. Hard.

I closed my mouth, dodging a putrid stink thick

enough to feel heavy against my skin. I knew the smell. Death. Nausea gripped my throat.

One quick glance told me the body was human, and there wasn't much left. I swallowed and dragged Forrest away from the stench.

She was shivering, her face so pale her skin looked almost blue. I led her by the hand back to the freshness of the creek and sat down next to her on a patch of soft grass. She curled into a tight knot, her arms wrapped around her legs, her face buried between her knees.

Finally recovering my own breath, I pulled my phone from my pocket. Not too wet. I wiped it on the front of my shirt and called 911.

****

"No, Gran. Sheriff Robb says I have to stay here." I glanced over at the dark-haired boy dumping water out of his soggy tennis shoes. He was making such a huge production out of not watching me. I even managed a brief smile.

"Are you okay, sweetie-pie?" Gran said. Her voice crackled over the poor connection.

"I'm fine. The sheriff wants to talk to us again after he and the other cops finish up with the…" A shiver grabbed my shoulders. "Uh…the body."

"I'll drive out there." A tinge of hysteria colored Gran's voice.

"No. Really. I'm safe. Just a little freaked."

"Well, all right. As long as Sheriff Rob is with you, I guess that's okay. I'll wait at home. Call me soon."

I clicked the phone off, gulped in additional air, and swallowed hard, hoping I wouldn't be sick again. I covered my face with my hands. God. The smell. Gross.

Even from this far away, the stench stung my senses, clinging to my clothing and my hair. I couldn't wait to get home and take a hot bath with every one of Gran's flowery soaps.

"Forrest?" His voice felt close, but he didn't touch me. Thank goodness. I'd probably incinerate.

I gave Josh a weak smile. "My gran, poor thing. She wants to drive over, but she'd never find us. Besides, it'll be dark soon."

He nodded and leaned his long frame on a nearby boulder. "Last thing we need is another lost hiker."

"Do you think that's what happened? Maybe the guy got lost?"

The boy shrugged one shoulder in a careful way. "Guy coulda fallen. Who knows? Little late for snakes."

"Snakes? Like rattlesnakes?" An icy shudder rippled through me. "Creepy, horrible snakes?"

"It's too cold now. Been a couple weeks since I've seen any diamondbacks."

"Ugh." I glanced up at the striped red and buff walls of the desert canyon, the lush green of the plants next to the creek, the bright colors of the changing sycamore leaves. "I loved this creek. It's the only green place in the whole valley. Now…" I dropped my chin onto my chest and sighed.

He moved closer, but left a space between us. His body blocked the wind, and I warmed up. I smiled to myself. Josh hadn't been more than three feet from my side since he found me screaming my lungs out.

He dodged my thank-you smile, found a small stick, and scratched figures in the sand.

I cocked my head to one side and finally drew in a clean breath. There was a quiet about him. A soothing quiet. More of the terror drained away.

While he wasn't looking my way, I studied his profile. He wasn't handsome. Yet. Someday his face would have good features, beautiful bronze skin, a powerful jaw, and strong, straight nose.

Right now, the rich, dark amber color of his eyes drew me. Made me want to know him better. He was the first person in this never-wanted-to-come-to-the-stupid-desert who'd even piqued my interest.

His wide mouth was pinched, pale at the sides. The dimple in his right cheek appeared and disappeared when the muscles in his jaw flexed. His forehead had a slight sheen of sweat. Straight, dark hair, still slightly damp, hid the tops of his ears, the nape of his neck, and his expressive brows.

I studied him. He didn't seem scared. Exactly.

Angry? Maybe, but there was something else too. I studied him more closely. The set of his shoulders was stiff, like he guarded a great sadness inside. Oh, God. Had he known the poor guy lying below the cliff?

Quietly, while the boy still wasn't facing my way, I held out my palm and opened my senses.

*So much sorrow. So much loneliness.*

His pain hissed against my skin and singed the sensitive tips of my fingers. I almost pulled back, but in spite of the increased tension in my brow, I continued to read his feelings.

He'd buried the pain deeply, covering it with layers of denial and bravado and courage. It was old pain, pain he'd coped with for years. Why?

He turned toward me, and I dropped my hand and rubbed it on my thigh, trying to appear nonchalant. Not wanting him to figure out I'd been staring, I glanced away. It just wouldn't be fair to dig any deeper. If we were to be friends, I needed to wait.

Everyone has secrets. I have more than my share. Curious as I was, I knew it was important to be patient and let him tell his story in his own time.

We heard something scuffling and grunting nearby and both shot to our feet. I moved closer to Josh, almost touching. Close enough to feel his warmth.

Two deputies hoisted an empty stretcher over the nearby log and, without comment, headed toward the cliff and the body.

No need to hurry.

An older, overweight man wearing a dress shirt and bolo tie scrambled panting between the rocks and a paloverde tree. Without a word, he followed the cops out of sight.

"He's Doc Howard," Josh said quietly after the man disappeared into the brush.

I glanced east, in the direction of the trailhead a quarter mile away. In the dusk, the bright blue lights of an ambulance flashed against the canyon walls.

The sunlight dipped below the cliffs, and the wind was cooler. I hugged my arms around my waist and wished I'd brought a jacket.

Josh untied his only slightly-damp sweatshirt and draped it over my shoulders.

"Thanks."

"Thought I told you not to talk to each other." Sheriff Robb scowled as he came around a scruffy pine. His cowboy boots were covered with mud, and the knees of his crisply pressed uniform were splotched with dirt.

"We didn't discuss anything important, sir," Josh

said.

The sheriff grunted and took off his hat. He brushed a hand through neatly trimmed, curly brown hair, and stopped a few feet in front of us. His weathered face was serious.

I swallowed hard and took a step back. The guy looked pissed.

"He's okay," Josh whispered in my ear.

A quick smile crinkled the corners of the sheriff's eyes in a reassuring way. I let out the breath I'd been holding, and my shoulders relaxed.

With a casual wave, the cop signaled me to sit. He took up a rock of his own. "Josh," he said, "witnesses need to be interviewed separately, but this has been a tough day for you two. I could take your statements here rather than going back to the station. Can you hang out down by the creek until I call you?"

Josh gave a quick nod and moved away without a word.

After the sheriff turned on a small recorder he'd pulled from his shirt pocket, he crossed one booted foot over his knee and leaned forward. "Ready?"

My stomach leaped into my throat, but I gave the man a nervous shrug and clenched my hands together.

He poked the record button. "Tell me again how you found the body." His voice was smooth, friendly, like he'd stopped to say hey on the main drag. He dug in his pocket, pulled out a bright red poker chip and fingered the disc casually.

Despite his smile, I shifted in place. My heartbeat had never quite slowed to normal, and now my pulse raced again. The log I was sitting on felt hard and cold and freaking uncomfortable.

I swallowed a few times. This was important. I closed my eyes to remember every detail. I wanted to be accurate. Wanted to be helpful. Most of all, I didn't want to come off like a dopey, teenage idiot.

Straightening my shoulders, I stuck out my chin to summon my gumption, and began the story. "I went for a hike up the creek. When it was time to go home, I headed back to Verde."

"When was this?"

"Uh…about four. I stayed after school for a bit. We start cross-country next week, and I needed to finish a history paper. I worked in the library. Gran wanted me home by seven, and it takes about an hour to get up the hill to Jerome."

"See anyone else on the trail?"

"Just Josh." I twirled my hair around my finger, but then dropped my hand and hissed under my breath. God. I must have looked like a total ditz with that move. "We talked for a few minutes, but I'd come alone."

The sheriff cocked his hat back. "Did you plan to meet here?"

"No," I said a little too loudly. I glanced down and lowered my voice. "I've seen him at school some, but we didn't talk until today."

Robb smiled and waited for me to continue.

I touched my hot cheeks with my palms, cleared my throat, and continued. "Like I said, we talked for maybe five minutes. I gave him a bottle of water and a cookie."

"What kind?"

I crinkled my brow. "Oatmeal. Why?"

The sheriff shrugged. "Details help."

"Then I was hiking back to the trailhead. To my jeep. I thought I saw a rabbit in the brush, and I went to find it. That's when I noticed the awful smell. Don't know how I missed it heading upstream."

Robb flipped his poker chip and then glanced at the sky. "Wind shifts in the late afternoon."

My heart was beating so hard, I thought I might dash under a bush like that stupid rabbit. The vision of the dead guy flooded back into my mind, and my stomach lurched again. Breathing through my nose, I held on…barely.

The sheriff whistled, and Josh appeared a moment later. When he put a hand on my shoulder, I let out a pent-up, can-we-get-this-over-with sigh.

"Was it a good cookie, Josh?" the sheriff asked.

"Yeah. I like oatmeal. Even the healthy kind her gran makes."

The sheriff tucked away his recorder.

"Do you know who the guy is?" Josh asked. "Has someone gone missing?"

The sheriff pocketed the chip and drew his fingers down the corners of his mouth. After a long moment, he shook his head. "Don't know of anyone."

I let my hair drape over my face. "Was it an accident? Did he d-die quickly?"

The man stood, stretching out his back. "Oh, he went quickly, all right." He signaled for them to follow him. "We'll know more soon. He was shot, probably before he fell. Been buried and then dug up by critters."

I shivered again and pulled the sweatshirt closer.

Josh took my hand.

"Murdered?" I whispered.

CHAPTER 4

Was Forrest avoiding me? For the past two days, I hadn't seen her, even though I searched for her between classes and after school. I walked across the high school quad and climbed the steps to the covered ramada everyone used as a lunch area. Maybe I'd spot her today.

I put down my sandwich and edged into the picnic table with the best view of the quad. I'd been excused five minutes early from English class, but she probably wasn't out of geometry yet.

I sat on the bench. For once, the table wasn't too hot to touch, and with the light breeze blowing between the low-built classrooms, the first cool day of fall made me smile.

There. Forrest entered the grassy area on the far side and walked across the green space, deep in conversation with a girlfriend. Jeans, sandals, and a Verde Valley High School rally shirt, just like every other girl.

Not.

She hadn't seen me yet, and my heart gave a what-do-I-do-now kick. Should I wave? Or chill?

Right below me, Forrest gave her friend a quick hug, and they split up. Her friend said something, waved, and hurried toward the library.

Before I could swallow the boulder in my throat

and find my voice, Dennis Robb sauntered past her, his gang of coyotes trailing in pack formation.

Dennis stopped.

Shit.

Whatever the creep said made Forrest mad. She tossed her bright hair like she didn't care, but her mouth was pinched, and her shoulders caved in.

The other boys quickly surrounded her.

What a bunch of jerks. I stood and headed for the steps.

"Heard you're working for my dad now." Dennis raised his voice loud enough for everyone in the quad to hear. "He said you did a great job finding that dead guy. Didja scream real loud?"

More hoots from the pack.

I booked it down the steps.

Dennis grinned. "'Course, Dad said the guy stunk to high heaven. Made you puke."

The boys laughed too loudly and jostled each other.

I pushed through the circle of shoulders and got between Forrest and Dennis. I spread my legs and squared my shoulders the way the sheriff did when he was ready to get tough. "Leave her alone."

It worked. Dennis stepped back, but then his mouth twisted into an ugly smile. "Ah-h-h. Now ain't that cute, guys?" he said in a high-pitched, sing-song tone to the pack mates next to him. "Little Joshie here wants to play super-dude."

I lowered my chin and stepped closer. My hands curled into fists, but I didn't raise them. Yet.

Forrest tugged my arm. "Come on, Josh. It's late. You gotta come see something in my jeep."

With my fists doubled so tight they ached, I locked

my knees and refused to budge. I glared at Dennis.

Dennis shrugged off his letter jacket and with that irritating asshole smirk of his, tossed it to his second.

I crouched and circled.

The pack moved back, giving us room to fight.

Watch. Next they'll be taking bets.

Forrest whirled to face me and grabbed my shoulders. "Please, Josh. Don't," she whispered next to my ear.

I let out a low growl, but relented, giving the creep one last I-could-take-you-anytime grimace.

Dennis shrugged. "Adios, Kwail. Or should I call you Chicken Little?" He flapped his elbows to imitate a bird and cackled. The pack joined in.

"Whipped," someone called.

"Oh. Shut. Up," Forrest shouted.

Almost blind with rage, I wanted to smash Dennis's ugly face, but Forrest dragged me by the hand out of the quad. The buck-buck-buck chicken calls made my teeth ache.

"What an asshole," she said under her breath.

"Has been for a while." I glanced over my shoulder. "Can't believe we were ever friends when we were kids."

"Sorry."

"He changed," I said with a shrug, "turned into the biggest bully around. We haven't hung out since I moved back from California, more than three years ago."

The anger roiling in my blood cooled enough for me to see where I was going. "I coulda taken him."

"And gotten expelled?"

I kicked a rock hard enough to make my big toe

ache. "Still, mighta been worth the trouble."

We hurried across the dusty student parking lot. Forrest stopped and gave me a thorough once-over, then shook her head. "BTW, I can take care of myself."

"Sure, sure. I know." I edged closer, caught a whiff of her perfume, and had to smile. "One-on-one, I would have let things play out. You could chew Dennis Robb up and spit him out in the dirt, even if the odds were pretty unfair."

She chuckled and flashed me a smile.

My insides felt buzzy and warm. Man, she could smile. I liked her smile almost as much as I liked her hair.

"Guess so," she said, pulling car keys out of her front jeans pocket.

I leaned against a nearby fence post while she stowed her backpack inside the ugliest car I'd ever seen. It was putrid pink and rusted, and someone had painted bright red polka dots all over the banged-up body. "Where'd you get this hunk o' junk?"

Forrest turned to face me, her expression frosty. "You got a car?"

I shut my trap and stepped out of range. Maybe she could've handled Dennis *and* his pack on her own.

"Well, do you?"

"Uh…" I cleared my throat. "No."

"Then don't dis mine." She stroked the door handle like the junker was precious. "I bought Tilley all by myself, with money I earned this summer washing dishes in a hideous Chinese restaurant."

I scratched my head and searched for something nice to say about the heap. "Uh, looks like an old tour jeep. One the fool tourists from Sedona ride around in to see the sights."

"It is." She stepped forward, her chin held high. The muscles in her jaw twitched. "And I'm proud of her. Took me a week to get all the red polka dots just perfect."

I choked back a snicker and threw up my hands. "Okay, okay. You drive the best damn jeep in the whole of Verde Valley."

She crossed her arms and glared at me again. Man. Her glare felt like a laser when she swept her eyes from my boots to my forehead.

I shrugged, and she smiled.

I grinned back. What a smile.

# CHAPTER 5

*Thursday, one week later*

I let the Trading Post's screen door slam behind me and tossed two bags of groceries on the kitchen table. I glanced at the clock. "Hey, George," I called through the curtain blocking our living area from the store. "Forrest will be here for dinner soon."

"Yeah. Be there in a minute."

Whistling, I lit the old gas stove with a match, and pulled down the iron skillet hanging over the sink. Chili. I chopped a big onion and slung the whole pile in the oil to sizzle. My mouth watered. Two cans of jalapenos should be enough to stir up some heat.

George pushed through the curtain and gave a quick nod. "Something arrived for you today."

"Yeah? What?"

George held out his weathered palm, and my heart did a quick flip. I dropped the spoon into the pan. The bone flute. The one the Magician played the other day by the creek.

"Uh-h." I swallowed the tightness in my throat. "Where'd you get that?"

"Found it on your pillow when I went to get a book from your room." George twisted his mouth into a grimace. "Belongs to the Magician, right?"

I nodded, but couldn't meet George's stern gaze.

"Have you seen him again?"

I brushed my hair out of my eyes and picked up the spoon before it was too hot to handle. "Hadn't in years. Then I saw him the day Forrest and I found the body. First time he's appeared since I went into his cave when I was twelve."

He crossed his arms. "You forgot to mention something like this?" His voice didn't sound pissed. Just surprised.

I shrugged, added the meat, and stirred the chili. "Been busy. When he showed up by the creek last week, he played that thing."

George's mouth drooped into a deep frown. "What song?"

"The one mom used to sing. You know." I took the small instrument and whistled out a few brief notes.

"You can play it?"

"Guess so. Doesn't seem very hard." I rubbed my fingertips over the finely inlaid turquoise and coral just below the mouthpiece and played the tune again.

One brow rose suspiciously, and George grunted. "It's a courting flute."

I blinked.

"You know, girlfriends…love?"

The screen door slammed, and Forrest walked into the kitchen. "Oh, pretty." She took the flute from my hand and blew into the mouthpiece a few times, but only an ear-piercing squeak came out.

She glanced up at me and then over at George. Her brow furrowed. "Did I get the wrong day? You did say Thursday, right? Chili?"

George cleared his throat. "Hi, Forrest. Nice to see you again. We were just solving a little mystery."

I recovered my voice. "Yeah, a mystery. We were

trying to figure out who left me this…uh…gift."

"…and why," George added under his breath.

"Nice gift." Forrest said as she returned the flute, moved over to the stove, and stirred dinner. "Looks kinda old."

George rubbed his chin and smiled at the girl. "It is."

Courting flute? I stole a glance at Forrest. Girlfriend, maybe. My heart did a little jump in my chest. But love?

To keep her from seeing my red face, I turned away, and stashed the flute in a locked cabinet in George's desk, and tossed him the key.

"What's it for?" she asked, dumping in the cans of tomatoes. The concoction hissed.

I shrugged, but heat still burned my ears. Maybe she'd move on to a different subject. I pointed to the chili. "Here, dump in these beans too."

A frown flashed across her face and was gone. "Ah. A secret."

Man, the girl was persistent. I dragged my fingers through my hair.

She gave an almost imperceptible nod. "A top secret, huh? Okay. You don't have to tell me." The corners of her mouth sagged a little, and she kept her gaze on the bubbling pot.

"No, it's… It's not…"

Someone pounded on the front door of the Trading Post, and I grabbed the chance to dodge her question. I loped between the cabinets of the darkened store and unlocked the door. "Hey, Sheriff."

"Josh." The man didn't return my smile. "Is your cousin here?"

"He's in the kitchen."

"Want some chili?" George called from the back of the store. "Josh's making a double batch."

"Not a social visit, I'm afraid, Kwail. Need to ask you some questions."

George came into the room, and the two men shook hands. "Sure."

"Did you find out about the dead guy?" Forrest asked, coming through the curtain. "Do you know who he was?"

The sheriff took off his hat. "We identified him late yesterday. Name was Abrams. Morty Abrams." He turned to George. "You knew him, right?"

George stood very still. "Only in passing."

"Wasn't he the guy…?" I began, but George shot me a quick shut-up-if-you-want-to-keep-breathing glance.

Robb carefully placed his hat on the front counter, spread his feet in a lawman stance, and settled his arms over his chest. "We found tools up on the cliff where Morty'd been tossed off. He'd been doing a little prospecting, hadn't he, George?"

"Wouldn't know 'bout that." George fiddled with his silver belt buckle, and perspiration dampened his forehead. "Everyone in Verde Valley knew Morty and that no-good buddy of his were stealing artifacts. The tribe's artifacts."

Robb stepped closer. "You argued with him at the tribal council meeting. What'd you say on the official record that night?"

George stared at the floor, and my stomach dropped down to the worn pine boards. I glanced back and forth between the two men. Why didn't George say something? Why didn't he defend himself?

George narrowed his dark eyes to meet the cop's gaze. "I said if I caught that thief raiding graves, I'd kill him."

With my heart pounding like the drummer in a heavy metal band, I stepped between my guardian and the sheriff. "My cousin wouldn't hurt anyone. You know that. Besides, he's been with me or in the store all month."

"The medical examiner says Abrams died at least six weeks ago. Can you alibi George then?"

"August?" I dropped my chin and choked down my spit. "I was in California visiting friends most of August."

"Where were you in mid-August, George?"

"In the desert," he whispered.

"It's his month for prayer," I argued. "He's the tribe's shaman."

Robb fitted his hat on his head and pulled a set of handcuffs from his duty belt. "Sorry, Josh. I don't have a choice here. George Kwail, I have a warrant. You're under arrest on suspicion of the murder of Morty Abrams."

"No, wait," I shouted, but a rush of blood buzzed in my brain. I couldn't move. Couldn't think of a way to stop what was happening.

Forrest squeezed my arm.

Mumbling George's Miranda rights, Robb clipped the handcuffs on him and led him toward the front entrance. George didn't struggle.

His brow furrowed, Robb glanced over at me. "Sorry, son. I have to follow the law. The DA thinks he has enough evidence to prosecute. I have a warrant to search the store and your rooms in the back. You'll need to leave. Get some clothes. Your books. I'll have social services arrange a foster…"

"No. No foster home. Please!" George shouted. "He's been through enough. Josh can move up with his Aunt Gina in Jerome until we get things worked out."

"I'll drive him up tonight," Forrest offered.

Robb hesitated a moment, nodded, then led George out the door.

George called over his shoulder to Forrest. "Take care of him."

"I will," Forrest said, still holding my hand.

****

Burned chili sat in the sink, and the stench of blackened onions hung in the small kitchen. I tossed a duffel on the floor and dumped my ass on a chair.

My stomach looped into another set of knots. Leaning back, I stared at the log ceiling and scrubbed my face with both hands.

Forrest entered quietly through the back door. "I brought my jeep around." She picked up my bag in one hand. "Don't you want to take more than this?"

I shook my head. "I'll be back in a day or two," I said with a bravado I wanted to believe. "George didn't murder anyone. Cops will catch who did this and let him go."

She chewed on her lip. "Why'd they think George did it in the first place?"

My stomach cinched tighter. I stood and paced the narrow room. "Morty was a grave robber."

Her brows raised in a questioning expression, so I continued. "He's a crook. Worse than a crook. He goes out in the dessert and steals artifacts. Petroglyphs,

35

pots…sacred burial things must remain where they have always been."

"That's illegal, right?"

"Oh, yeah."

"You sell Native American artifacts in your store."

"We trade legal artifacts only. Things of the living, things found on private lands. New things made by the tribe. Never grave goods. Never sacred things. Morty would sneak out at night and steal from federal land. And our reservation."

"And somebody caught him." Forrest rubbed her hands on her upper arms as if she'd felt a cold draft.

"Not George," I said. "Sure, George was mad at him. Furious. The whole council was. George told me over the phone about the meeting. Man, he was so pissed, but my cousin could never kill anyone."

Forrest studied my face, and then for a long moment she lost focus, as though she was lost somewhere. I scratched the sudden itch crawling up the back of my neck. I got creeped out just standing there, waiting for her to say something more.

Then she blinked and grinned at me. "Okay. So we need to figure this out, but first, let's drive up to Jerome before it's too dark. Gran says you can come to dinner. Then we'll drop you at your Aunt Gina's. Did you call her?"

I grunted an affirmative and followed Forrest to the door. The deputy standing guard tipped his hat and allowed her to pass.

When I grabbed the doorknob to pull it shut, I glanced back into my room and froze. Ice, then scorching heat flashed over me. The Magician stood by my bed, beckoning to me.

With my heart beating near the top of my throat, I called to Forrest, trying not to let my voice break. "I-I forgot my phone. Be out in a minute."

I stomped into the bedroom, stood nose to nose with the ghost and glared. "Why'd you let the sheriff take George? You know he's innocent."

The Magician turned and sat on the bed. The mattress didn't squeak.

I leaned against the opposite wall and hugged my arms across my chest, gripping my elbows.

The ghost was still, as if he was waiting.

I rolled my eyes. "Damn. I get it."

I sat on the floor and calmed my thoughts, taking lighter breaths, in and out. Finally, the anger churning in me diffused enough for me to think. "What should I do?"

The Magician handed me the bone flute.

"Take it with me?"

An image pushed against my mind. I closed my eyes and denied the vision. "I can't. Not now."

The vision surrounded me. There would be no violence, no pain in what I saw. And yet my heart still pounded as I lowered my carefully-built barriers and allowed the Magician to share a vision with me.

*An eagle flew across the bright sky, and its long wing feathers whispered in the light wind. The smell of fresh water overlaid the dry air of summer.*

*Below, the desert stretched out in all directions, limitless. No roads scarred its surface, but a green river knifed through the barren land.*

*Ahead, a city had been built into the steep walls of a narrow river canyon.*

*People.*

*I looked closer.*

*People from a different time. Some worked in the fields nearby, gathering the crops. A woman with a water jar on her head climbed a steep trail to the dwelling in the cliff above.*

*With a long cry, the eagle banked its wings and turned into the sun.*

*A man glanced up and noticed the bird. He smiled, and worked a feather design into the earthen pot in his hands.*

*"Patience,"* whispered the Magician, more *a thought than a word. "Patience, like the eagle circling on the wind. Find your gift. Then you will help all the people."*

I let the muscles in my shoulders relax. When my heart slowed to normal, I opened my eyes.

I sat alone.

CHAPTER 6

The wheels of Forrest's dorky pink jeep skidded on the gravel shoulder of the cliff road. I gritted my teeth and grabbed the chicken bar. "You drive like a maniac," I shouted over the wind.

Forrest laughed, punched the gas pedal, and the tires squealed in protest around the next curve.

Eyes straight ahead, I told myself. Eyes straight ahead or I'd puke for sure. *Oh, shit. Here comes another hairpin turn.* I glanced over the barren edge of the road and gulped. Had to be a thousand feet straight down.

With a quick jerk, Forrest turned the wheel and rescued us from oblivion.

"Does your grandmother know you drive like this?" I groaned out.

"Sure. She taught me."

I pushed my body back against the bucket seat and braced for the next curve. The good news was the town of Jerome was only a few more torturous turns up the narrow, winding road. Maybe I'd live to be sixteen after all.

Above us, the tiny ghost town clung to the cone-shaped mountainside. Built a hundred years ago over a copper mine, several of the old buildings hadn't managed to hang on. A trail of broken timbers and brick tumbled down the steep slope.

Pillars of cement and steel still held the few newer structures in place. Hippies rediscovered the abandoned mining town way back in the sixties, and it had recently been revived as a tourist trap.

I liked going to the hamburger joint in town, but the art galleries and tourist junk were stupid. Besides, this was Dennis Robb's turf.

I stayed in the Valley, and only came to visit Aunt Gina and her husband, Rocky, when George wheedled me into being polite. Mostly I avoided the ghost town, the creep, and his gang of friends.

With one last stomach-twisting turn, the incline leveled off, and we drove down the narrow street at the bottom end of town. Forrest whipped the jeep into a parking spot on the side of the road.

The buzz of adrenaline drained from my fingertips, my body, my brain. I sucked in air and stared out across the infinite expanse of canyons and mesas stretching below the mountain.

"I'm worried about George," I said, more to myself than to her.

Forrest grabbed my bag from the back seat. "Didn't your aunt say she'd bail him out tomorrow morning?"

"Yeah." I swung my book bag over one shoulder.

"So relax. Like you said, the cops made a big mistake."

Nodding, I used the windshield to pull myself upright and jumped down from my seat. I shook the cramp out of my right hand and glanced up at the old clapboard building. "Is this your Gran's place?"

"Yeah," Forrest drew out the word to sound like a challenge and twisted her mouth to one side. "We live upstairs."

The neon pink sign over the door read:

Angel's Cloud

Psychic readings. Aura Photographs. Spiritual Guidance.

Forrest opened the pale blue door, and a string of Tibetan bells chimed. She shouted, "Hey, Gran."

I followed her through the jumbled, one-room store. Crystals, prayer sticks, incense. We climbed the narrow stairs at the back. "Weird. Feels like I've been here before."

"Probably have. We rent the store from your Aunt Gina. Place used to be her tattoo parlor."

Sudden cold made my teeth chatter, and creepy crawlies danced on my spine. I grunted with surprise. Why was I so spooked?

"Hi, Forrest, baby. Is that poor Joshie with you?" a woman's high voice echoed down from the top of the stairway.

Joshie? I grimaced but kept climbing. Even when I pulled up the hoodie of my jacket, I was still freezing.

We reached the top step.

"Oh, you poor, dear lamb. I've been waiting so long to meet you." A tiny woman wearing an oversized blue caftan floated toward me. Her fair skin was lined with tiny crinkles. Softly curled gray hair framed her face. "Forrest, darling." She said in a high-pitched voice. "Please get this lovely boy some of my special herbal tea."

"He's fine, Gran."

I mounted the last step, dropped my school pack, and glanced around. The smell of incense peeled the inside of my nose. I tried breathing through my mouth, but the overwhelming sweetness choked me. I coughed and cleared my throat quietly.

Flooded with evening light, the room was filled with warmth and soft furniture. Everything was pale blue. Blue curtains, blue rug, blue paintings on blue walls. My shoulders relaxed. The stench faded.

"Here, Joshie. Sit here, dear." The woman drew me to the wooden table in the center of the room and patted me on the shoulder. "I'll go get the dinner I cooked for you, dear boy. Later, we can talk."

I did as I was told.

She patted my shoulder. "When Forrest explained to me what happened, I went right in and made us a healthy kale and Brussels sprout soup, with lots of ginseng in the broth to boost your spirits."

"Uh, thanks. Ms…"

"Call me Angel Wings, darling." The woman fluttered out of the room.

Forrest rolled her eyes as she set a steaming mug of something foul-smelling in front of me. "That's her new name. She doesn't think her real name, Goldie Morgan, will get her much business." With a quiet smile, Forrest joined me at the table.

"Is she…uh, you know…a psychic? Like the sign says," I asked under my breath.

Forrest gave a disgusted-sounding snort, then glanced over her shoulder and lowered her voice. "She couldn't psych her way out of a Wal-Mart shopping bag."

I chuckled.

Forrest flipped her hair, and her expression softened. "She means well, and she's very good at listening to people's troubles. She gives them basic advice, but makes the whole thing sound"—Forrest held her fingers in an air quote—"mystical."

"What about you?"

"Me?" Forrest shook her head and glanced out the front window. "I don't believe in that shit."

My stomach tumbled down the steps I'd just climbed. I searched her face but only saw disdain. "Some people do have special talents." I said.

She shrugged.

My jaw clenched. Whether they wanted those talents or not.

Forrest stared over my head and drummed her fingers on the table. "I guess. Mostly it's just another way to con people." Looking even more disgusted, she waved a hand and sauntered into the kitchen. "Gran? Is dinner ready yet?"

I waited in the cool, placid room. Kale and brussel sprout soup? My stomach rumbled. How bad could it be?

I rapped a quick beat on the edge of the table. When sudden heat burned my fingers, I ripped my hands away. I glanced over one shoulder and grimaced. Something didn't make sense here. What was wrong with this place?

Carefully, I laid both hands on the table's rough wooden surface.

The overly sweet smell changed.

*The room reeked of choking dust and mildew. The light seemed different, too. Dim. With lots of shadows.*

I pulled my hands back again, but my heart was pounding so hard I felt my pulse in my ears.

No. I'd stopped these terrifying visions years ago. My mentor, Norah, taught me to shield myself from knowing. From seeing. From feeling.

I wanted to be normal. I wanted to live without the horrible sights that haunted me when I was a little kid.

I shivered.

Even after moving my chair away from the table and focusing my shields, the vision crowded my eyes and overwhelmed my defenses.

*My bare feet were cold. I stood by the window, peering through the ragged curtains at a woman below. Did I know her?*

*Yes. My friend Norah stood in the street, but why had she come all this way? To rescue me?*

*I raised my hand and tried to call out, but a loud voice boomed over my head.*

*My heart squeezed down into a tiny, racing bug. I dodged the fists aimed at me, scooted into a corner, and grabbed my quilt.*

*A woman screamed. "No, Kenny. Don't hit him again."*

*Pain. Anger.*

"Josh?" Forrest's voice. I surfaced for a minute, but was sucked back into the vision.

*Terror. I huddled in the corner, tasting blood on my swollen tongue. Sweat dripped off my nose, and more puddled under my armpits. I closed my eyes and prayed I wouldn't piss myself.*

Warm hands pulled me away.

"Josh?"

I struggled to focus on Forrest's pretty face.

Heaving an urgent breath, I jumped to my feet, dumping the chair on its side. The clatter echoed in the room, startling me, out of place in the peacefulness of the quiet blue space.

"Josh, what's wrong?"

I choked out her name.

Now she sounded frightened, but behind her soft light filled the space, and the scent of sandalwood tickled my nose. The terrible pain subsided.

"What happened? Are you sick?" She took a step closer, reaching for me.

I shook my head, unwilling to meet her frightened gaze. "It's nothing." My voice cracked, like I'd been strangled with powerful hands.

"Nothing? You're soaking wet." She didn't touch me again, but folded her arms and narrowed her scrutiny to my face. She didn't blink. Didn't twist her mouth in disgust. She studied me almost...almost like she understood.

My heart slowed to double time, and I picked the chair up off the floor, more as a distraction than to be polite. "Sorry. I guess you'd call this post-traumatic stress disorder."

She gave that snort again.

I turned my back to her and walked to the front window. I was taller now. Tall enough to see out the top half of the squeaky-clean glass. Before, my view had been blocked by a layer of grime.

"I remembered something," I said. "When I was a kid, my uncle hid me here."

Forrest joined me, still not touching, but her warmth flowed across the distance between us. "It's okay. George warned me when I dropped by last week. He thought I should know before you came to visit."

I cringed and dug my hands deeper into my pockets. "He shoulda kept his mouth shut."

She gave a shrug and turned me toward her. Placing one hand on my chest, she smiled up into my face. The green flecks danced in her eyes. "You're safe here."

I reached out and touched her hair. Silky. In the soft evening light, the strands turned gold, then copper, between my fingers.

My heart started pounding again, but it was different this time. I wanted to taste her lips. I moved my face closer, and her breath tickled my chin.

"He-ere, we go-o-o," Angel Wings—or whatever her crazy name was—called from the kitchen entrance.

I jumped back at least a foot, tripped, and almost landed on my butt.

Forrest dropped her hand and giggled.

"You're ab-so-*lute*-ly going to lo-ove this soup." Carrying in the huge bowl of green goo, Angel Wings didn't seem to notice our reactions. Or if she did, she didn't care that I'd almost kissed her granddaughter.

Wow. My neck and then my face heated with embarrassment. Even my scalp burned, but I stuffed my hands in my pockets again and beamed. *Almost kissed.*

I tried twice to swallow the king-sized furry hairball blocking my throat. Finally I gave up and walked over to the table. I could sit there now. I reinforced my shields with Forrest's smile and ate.

If I swallowed fast, the soup wasn't bad. It tasted green, but hot and spicy, too.

Angel Wings grinned when I asked for a second

bowl. Taking the chair next to me, she leaned her elbows on the table and spoke quietly in my ear. "Did my darling granddaughter tell you the story about how she was named Forrest?"

"Gran, puh-lease." Forrest drew out the complaint. "Don't bore Josh with our ridiculous family tale."

The woman rocked in her chair, still grinning. With her shoulders scrunched up to her ears, she appeared pleased with herself. Angel Wings had the same blue eyes and almost the same smile as Forrest, the same I-don't-give-a damn-what-you-think attitude.

"Did she tell you her mama, my daughter, lived in a tree for almost a year?"

I swallowed. "No, ma'am." This should be good.

Forrest groaned and kept her eyes on her soup.

I glanced back and forth between them. Might be worth hearing the story, just to watch my girlfriend squirm.

I froze, mid-slurp. Girlfriend? I watched her pretty, blushing face and smiled to myself. Yes. I wanted Forrest to be my girlfriend, and I was almost positive she liked me, too. My smile widened.

I still needed to kiss her to make it official. I set down my spoon, took a piece of soft wheat bread and buttered it. I leaned back until the chair creaked under me and waited for Angel Wings to continue.

She folded her hands. "Angie was nineteen. My daughter was an environmentalist, and wanted to protect the old-growth redwoods in northern California." She nodded to herself, her face serious. "It was so-o-o important for our planet to protect the trees from being logged. Ever. She made a commitment. She would stay in one of the ancient trees for a whole year."

With her elbows on the table, Forrest rested her head in her palms. She didn't even glance at either of us, but muttered something under her breath.

Angel Wings leaned in closer. "About a month later, she found out she was…" she dropped her gaze and lowered her voice to a whisper "…expecting."

Another groan from across the table.

"I wanted her to come down, but she was so stubborn."

"Wonder where she got that from?" Forrest hissed.

Angel Wings tossed off the comment with a flip of her hand. "Forrest's father tried to talk Angie down, too. So did the authorities, but no one could convince her. Angie made a promise, and she was healthy, so she stayed in the tree. We Morgan women can be rather pushy broads."

Forrest rubbed her eyes with the heels of her palms. "Ya think?"

"A doctor who was part of the movement climbed up once a month and made sure she was fine. Her father built her a warm, dry shelter. Her supporters made sure she had plenty to eat. We came to visit as often as we could." Angel Wings' face glowed with a faraway expression. "Such a lovely place to grow a baby. So peaceful. So spiritual."

"Oh." I sat straighter and nodded. "Forrest. I get it. You were born up there?"

The little lines around Angel's bright eyes crinkled with her smile. "Angie meant to come down. She'd promised me she would, but the contractions started several weeks early, in the middle of the night. The doctor barely got there in time."

"Wow. Born in a giant redwood?"

Forrest gave a quick nod from behind her hands.

"I like the name. It means something."

She huffed and folded her arms on the table. "Better than Spotted Owl."

Her grandmother's brow wrinkled. "That would have been a silly name."

"And Forrest isn't?"

"The name fits you." I turned and gave her hand a squeeze. "It's original, like you."

Forrest crossed her eyes and stuck her tongue out. "I guess. At least my nickname isn't Hoot."

## CHAPTER 7

Later that night Forrest drove me up the hill to Rocky and Gina's place. All the way there, she sang loudly and a little off-key to the old song, "Where's the Love?" by the Black Eyed Peas. She left the jeep running while I grabbed my duffel in the back seat.

I glanced around the busy street, and my stomach dropped to the rusty floorboards. Damn. I wanted to kiss Forrest good night, but the bar was overflowing with customers, and several tough-looking dudes hung out on the sidewalk, smoking and sipping their brews.

Last thing I needed were witnesses to my first attempt.

I hopped out and slammed the door. "Well...later," I said with a grunt.

For an instant, disappointment flickered over her face. Then her smile returned, brighter than ever. "I can pick you up for school in the morning," she called through the jeep's open window.

"Uh..." I scrambled around in my brain for any excuse. No way would I ride that crazy road again in her pink-polka-dot-terror-machine. "We have cross-country practice tomorrow. It'll be dark by the time we're finished. You'll be tired, so let's take the late bus back up the mountain."

Forrest shrugged one shoulder. "'kay. See ya at the bus stop.

"Yeah. See ya at seven."

Revving Tilley, she waved and took off. At the end of the block, the jeep sputtered and backfired. A cloud of black smoke shot out the tail pipe.

I shook my head. Man, that hunk-of-pink-'n-red-junk needed some work. She'd never let me tinker on the old heap alone, but I could teach her how to clean the spark plugs and tune it, at least.

I walked through the open door of Rocky's Roost, and the smell of stale liquor and sweat smacked me in the face. Country swing blared over the speakers, and a biker couple in leather and studs danced hip to hip in slow circles in the center of the room. Aunt Gina glanced up from pulling a beer and grinned. "You made it."

Rocky, her new husband, laid a basket of garlic fries in front of an old cowboy and wiped his hands on his apron. "Hey, Josh. You doin' okay?"

"Worried about George." I grabbed a bag of chips from the display hooks behind the counter and ripped it open.

Gina squeezed her brightly painted lips together and shoved her blond bangs out of her eyes. "George would never hurt anyone. He'll probably be released by morning. Rocky's already talked to the sheriff."

I gave a quick nod, and the constriction around my heart eased off.

Gina raised the wood counter and walked out from behind the enormous, ornate bar. She put her arm around my waist, probably because she wasn't tall enough to reach her hands over my shoulders anymore.

She studied my face, her blue eyes full of concern. "Your room's ready. Go on down and get settled."

"Thanks." I pushed through the swinging doors into the kitchen, and made my way out to Sam's neatly tended garden behind the building. I clomped down the steep wooden stairway to their little house.

The door stood half open. I dropped my duffel on the couch and checked out the fridge. Milk. I grabbed the half-empty gallon. Fresh chocolate chip cookies cooled on a cookie sheet. I stacked six together and kicked back in Sam's recliner by the picture window. The town of Camp Verde spread out below, twinkling in the dark night.

The cookies burned my tongue. I chewed carefully, alternating with a long draw of milk cool to my mouth. Two more big ones should hold me a while. I headed for the kitchen at the same time Rocky walked through the door.

The man filled the space. Well over six-six, with shoulders like bulldozers, and wicked tats covering most of his arms, he could have been scary, except for the puppy dog expression on his face.

"Sheriff Robb called me back."

I tensed.

Rocky held up his huge palms. "Relax, Josh. George is fine. They didn't transfer him over to the county jail. Sheriff says he needs to check out a few things. They'll keep him in a holding cell in Verde for the night."

"Can he come home tomorrow?"

"Investigation probably won't be done until at least Monday. We'll work on bail. Robb seems to think the judge will release him then."

My gut ached. I grimaced and slammed a fist onto the counter. "Man. That sucks. He has to stay in jail all weekend?"

"Not so bad. Go visit him tomorrow after school. Bring him some books."

I blew a long breath at the ceiling. "I don't understand any of this."

Rocky thumped me on the shoulder. "I need to talk to the Sheriff tomorrow anyway. Sometimes I hear rumors when I'm pouring at the bar."

"Yeah?"

"Been a black market for artifacts around here for years. Everyone knew Morty was in on the deal." Rocky triple-stacked some cookies, bit down, but continued to talk. "For a guy who never worked, he always had way too much money for booze and drugs."

"Do you know who killed him?"

"Nope." Rocky's dark eyes narrowed and slid back and forth a few times. "He hung with some out-of-town guys about the time he disappeared. Already told Robb."

I turned toward my room, my shoulders aching, my head pounding.

Rocky drummed his beefy fingers on the counter. "One other thing, Josh."

When I glanced back, Rocky didn't meet my gaze. The cookies roiled in my stomach. More bad news?

"I couldn't figure out why Robb arrested George on such flimsy evidence, so I pushed him when we spoke on the phone. Turns out, he found one other piece of evidence he didn't mention at the trading post. DA wanted to keep it a secret until discovery, but Robb wasn't happy about it."

I gritted my teeth. "A gun?"

"No, no gun, but I guess when they examined the

body, they found part of an eagle feather in the dead guy's hand."

"No one can own an eagle feather, except..." The world dimmed. I closed my eyes and held on to the counter.

"Yeah," Rocky let out an enormous sigh and lumbered to the door. "No one can possess an eagle feather except a shaman."

****

The run after school on Friday felt good. Pounding six miles through the desert cleared my mind, loosened the tense muscles in my shoulders and back and legs. After a long, hot shower, I dressed, rubbed my wet hair with a gym towel, and tossed the rag in the team hamper. I'd wait for Forrest by the library.

She was already there. I grinned and trotted the rest of the way to the bench where she sat. Too bad her damp hair was tangled into a messy knot at the nape of her neck. I wanted to pull my fingers through the soft strands again. Maybe touch her face.

She jumped up and took a step closer, giving me a once-over with her blue-green eyes. My skin heated.

"Hey, Josh. What's that goofy look on your face?"

My heart raced like I'd finished an hour of wind sprints. I stared at the tarmac, but the tops of my ears still burned. "Nothin'," was all I managed to force out.

She gave my hand a tug. "The bus is almost ready to leave."

"Uh, yeah." I drew her closer to me, and she moved into my arms like she belonged there. She was soft and warm, and smelled like girl's shampoo and flowers.

Forrest grinned up at me and touched my mouth

with one finger. "Let's sit in the back of the bus." Her hands did amazing things to the back of my neck, and for a moment I couldn't remember my name.

I pulled her down on the bench. As much as I wanted to touch her, I'd better blurt out my plan quickly, or I'd totally forget what I had to do. "Forrest, I need to go see George."

"Okay." She cuddled up next to me. "I'll call my gran and come with you."

"No. Listen. I have to talk to him. Alone."

The green flecks in her eyes stood out against the blue. They always did when she was thinking. After a long moment, she nodded. "Sure. You'll be all right getting home?"

"Yeah. Rocky'll pick me up." I let out the breath I'd been holding for the last infinity and beyond. "You're not mad?"

She shot me a derisive twist of her mouth. "Josh. I get it. George is your family. Don't worry about me. Text me if you learn anything important."

"Sure, but let's be careful what we say in public."

Her eyes lit. "Do we need a code? Like in a spy novel?"

"This is not a spy novel, but I do need to find out what's going on."

"We could be detectives," she said, and grabbed my arm.

"Not really.

"We could still be sneaky? Right?"

I gave her a leery look. You know, eyes squinted, brows down.

"We'll invent special names, like they do on military operations. I'll be Red Dog, and you can be

Hawkeye."

I laughed for the first time in days. "I think you're mixing up *Star Wars* and the old re-runs of *M.A.S.H.*"

"Okay, okay. When you visit George, tell Sheriff Robb we want to help with the investigation."

I rubbed my nose with two fingers, rolling her suggestion around in my brain. I'd known the sheriff for years, almost forever. Robb was one of the good guys. He even coached Little League one year, back when Dennis and I were friends.

No. Robb was an adult, and sheriff no less. No way he'd want a couple kids sneaking around doing their own detective work. "We better keep this between us."

When Forrest opened her mouth to object, I put up my hand. "Just for now. Just until we find some proof of George's innocence."

Her expression grew more skeptical.

"Forrest, look, this case is about more than the murder of a local scumbag. Even if George hadn't been accused of murder, we'd still need to find out what's going on."

She nodded, but a frown still pulled on her beautiful mouth.

I grabbed her hand and held on. "This is about my tribe. My heritage."

She seemed to think about it, and my heart thumped in my chest, hard, harder. Then she gave me a full smile, eyes and lips and body.

I let out a pent-up breath I hadn't known I was holding.

Behind us, the bus driver jumped aboard and started the engine. The last stragglers ran for their ride.

She gave me a quick salute. "Orders understood,

Colonel Mustard."

I brushed my lips against her soft cheek. She smelled so good. "Later, Miss Scarlet."

## CHAPTER 8

I paced the sheriff's office, waiting for George to be brought up from the holding cells in the basement. Seemed like ages since I saw my cousin. I twisted my hands and then hid them in my pockets. At least I didn't have to go down into the dungeon to visit him.

The doorknob rattled, and George sauntered in with a smile on his face, looking like he just came in from his Friday night poker game.

"Josh," he exclaimed. "Thanks for coming."

Robb gave us a high sign. "I'll give you guys a few minutes."

I wasn't sure what to say, but nodded and handed over the stack of mysteries Rocky sent.

"You should have gotten me *Birdman of Alcatraz*," George said with a straight face. Then he laughed. "Man, you should see your expression."

I let out a long groan, and George opened his arms. We hugged, slapping each other hard on the back. I brushed something out of my eyes. "I've been worried about you."

George's face flickered with concern, but then he grinned. "I'm okay for now, kiddo. I'm innocent."

"I know."

George took me gently by the shoulders, tipped his head, and studied my expression closely. "Do you?"

"Of course."

"Good. The sheriff's working on some other theories of the murder."

I threw myself down on one of the chairs in front of Robb's wide, cluttered desk. I scratched my nails through my hair until my scalp hurt. "Then why won't he let you come home?"

"Not up to him. He's on our side, but he has to follow what that jackass district attorney tells him." George eased into the heavy chair next to mine. "You doing okay at Gina and Rocky's?"

"Yeah, sure."

"How's Forrest?"

I glanced up. "She's fine." I said coolly, even though heat singed my cheeks and the tops of my ears.

"M-m-m," said George. "Better than fine. Good. You need a friend right now."

A quiet knock came through the flimsy panel door, and Robb peeked his face in. "Brought you guys some dinner."

I glanced up in surprise as the sheriff unloaded thick sandwiches and cold sodas from a takeout carton onto his desk.

"See," George chuckled and held up his dinner. "I'm doing fine. Relax. This will all be behind us soon."

I bit into the roast beef sandwich and chewed. Mustard, pickles, some awesome cheese. I hadn't realized how hungry I was. I stuffed another bite into my mouth.

The sheriff pulled out his rolling chair and sat behind his desk. Leaning back, he took a long draw on his soda and agreed with George. "We gotta wait for that idiot, wet-under-the-saddle DA to come to his senses. Judge Hawkins'll set him straight next week."

"Then why…?"

Robb stared me straight in the eye. "There's not enough evidence to hold George over for trial, much less prosecute him. Really, Josh. But our fresh-out-of-night-school DA has a burr up his…."

George grunted.

"Sorry," the sheriff added. "Pisses me off."

Robb dug in his pocket and pulled out his hundred-dollar poker chip. He flipped it a couple times in the air, catching the red disc with one hand. He seemed to be thinking.

I waited.

The man straightened his wide shoulders until they stretched his neatly pressed uniform. "Sure, an alibi would help, but George doesn't have a motive for killing Morty any jury is going to buy. And there's no physical evidence other than a few odd sprigs of a feather. All circumstantial. No fingerprints. No weapon. Nothing to tie George to the case other than one stupid…"

George grunted again to interrupt him.

"It was stupid, man. You can't go around threatening people. Even scumbags like Morty."

George dropped his chin to his chest. "Yeah, I know."

\*\*\*\*

A couple hours later, I climbed down from the high seat of a beat-to-shit dump truck and waved to the driver. "Thanks, Circe."

The old man gave me a halfhearted salute with his battered cowboy hat, ground the gears, and took off down the dusty desert road back toward town.

Engulfed in a cloud of blue exhaust, I coughed, but waited until the truck was over the next rise before I headed cross-country the last few miles to the mine. The attendant at the gas station near the highway must have turned on the lights. The florescent bulbs flickered and sent long, creepy shadows across the desert.

I winced and crushed a twist of guilt. I told George I was headed back to Jerome to visit Forrest tonight. That was a lie.

I lied to Forrest, too, saying I would bunk this evening at the Trading Post. I kicked a rock out of my path. More lies to Gina and Rocky.

Mom always said if you lie, you'd better have a good memory. Too bad. Tonight no one could know where I was going.

After ducking under the barbed wire fence next to the dirt road, I hiked over the barren land. Long shadows stretched across the rocky hills.

Nothing much grew around here, not even the tall agave plants littering the rest of the high desert. Too much salt. Even the sagebrush and mesquite were stunted.

I glanced at the sky to check the time. Must be almost seven. The sun set twenty minutes ago, and only a rim of orange light glowed in the western sky.

Right now I could see my way, but in another half hour, it would be so dark I wouldn't be able to find my own backside, much less the salt mine. Better hurry.

Trotting up the next rise, I surveyed the small valley below and then let out a long, relieved sigh.

No one around.

Not that anyone ever hung out here. The whole town knew about the ancient mines, but they were nothing more than holes in the ground. They'd been boarded up for centuries. They were dangerous. And perfect for hiding a secret.

I slid down the last hill, my shoes crunching over salt-encrusted gravel. At the third Danger sign in from the rock pile, I climbed over a few boulders and yanked off the rotted boards blocking the entrance.

Nothing had disturbed my hiding place. The tiny scrap of orange plastic under the termite-chewed plank was still there. I glanced around one last time, my quick breaths fogging in the cooler night air.

Flipping on the small flashlight I always carried in my backpack, I leaned into the black space. The entrance was narrow, so I guerrilla-crawled on my elbows and belly for fifty feet. Gravel gouged my arms and knees, and salt dust stung my eyes. The quiet pounded against my ears.

I shoved several large boulders out of the way and squeezed through the opening into the large cavern. I stood and stretched, brushing the white dust off my clothes. The cave was dry, no dripping water. No rain this month.

I found my cache of supplies behind some old timbers. Soon I had more light and a long drink of bottled water. I could eat the dried food I stored here for emergencies, but I still had half a sandwich tucked in my pack.

Dumping my backpack next to me, I crossed my legs and leaned against the cool wall of the mine. My stomach growled. I'd eat first, then double-check the treasure. I bit into my sandwich and chewed.

\*\*\*\*

"For-r-rest," Gran called from the bottom of the

stairs. I looked up from stirring tofu into the brown rice and veggies and wrinkled my nose. What I wouldn't give to drop by the Haunted Hamburger for a double beef cheeseburger with extra fries and chocolate cheesecake with whipped cream. I let out a long, dying-for-junk-food sigh. Maybe I could meet Josh there sometime. Listen to the crazy band who played on Friday nights.

I sighed again. Josh said he was staying in Verde tonight, but I could sneak out after dinner for a slice of chocolate cheesecake anyway.

Gran floated into the room. Today's caftan was a migraine-inducing pink. She'd done her hair up in a scarf like she was some sort of far-eastern swami, and enormous gold earrings dangled to her shoulders. I tried not to make a face, but she looked ridiculous.

Sharp twinges of guilt pinched at my heart. Gran was doing everything she could to take care of us. She had a client coming for a Tarot reading in half an hour, and needed to dress the part. If she got a good tip, there would be enough to make the overdue rent.

I dumped our dinner in a chipped bowl and gave a quick sigh. Nobody else cared about us. Mom was…I swallowed quickly. Mom was gone. And Dad? He'd never been around. What a deadbeat.

I pushed back my anger, smiled at Gran, and gave her a hug. I'd wear the ridiculous outfit myself if I thought I could pull off a reading without laughing out loud.

Gran gave me a quick kiss on the cheek. "This smells wonderful, honey. Thanks for cooking."

I pulled up a chair, but I wasn't hungry, and only fiddled with my food. I tapped my fork against the plate a few times and then smiled.

Maybe I could get a job after school. The Connor Hotel just put a Help Wanted sign in the window. I took a bite of tofu. I'd skip the cheesecake and talk to the manager tonight.

CHAPTER 9

*Wearing his new eagle feather, the Apprentice paced in front of the meager fire. His stomach ached with hunger. It had been two days since he'd eaten more than a handful of dried corn.*

*With little rain this year, the crops had failed. The children grew too thin, their eyes dull with starvation. Many of the women died.*

*He had danced. He had prayed. As shaman, he had offered the sacrifices the Magician taught him to offer, but the spirits had abandoned them.*

*He crouched and rubbed his hands over his face. The people looked to him for leadership, but he had failed. They muttered in small groups. They watched him, their eyes full of fear. How could he save them?*

*Now the elders were discussing whether to use the sacred water from the well for irrigation. If all the people worked quickly to dig a canal, they might save the crop. Save some of the people from starvation. Save the tribe.*

*There was danger in this plan. How many times had the Magician told him to leave the sacred well for the spirits to drink? Should they disobey the Magician? Disobey the spirits?*

*Fear for his people weighed heavily in his heart. When he stirred the fire, a few sparks rose into the starlit night.*

*He stood. He would go to the Magician's grave. He would find a way.*

My chin dropped onto my chest, and the movement woke me with a start. I shook off the weird dream and sat up, but I bumped the side of my head on the rough cave wall. Damn. That hurt.

I picked up the flashlight beside me and searched the space. How long had I been asleep? Was it morning?

Stretching, I rubbed the sore spot on my temple until the pain stopped, and then crawled partway down the entrance. No. Still dark outside, but the moon had risen, and it cast long shadows over the hillside.

"Watch out," called a deep male voice in the distance.

I froze, and my heart pounded like the jackrabbit I trapped once but let go when I saw the terror in the poor thing's eyes.

"Yeah, yeah. Damn stuff's heavy." Another voice. Closer this time. Louder.

Whoever was out there wasn't worried about being heard. I fumbled to switch off my light and lay as still as that frightened rabbit.

Were the strangers headed toward me? Should I crawl farther back in the mine and hide? I chewed on my salty lips and leaned forward instead, straining to listen.

Now the voices sounded much farther away, and I couldn't understand the words. In slow motion, I moved toward the narrow opening. I was used to the dim light, so I saw the shadows of the men clearly.

Two—no, three—big guys. And a truck. No headlights. A few flashlight beams danced around the entrance to the smaller mine below me. The men hadn't spoken again.

I let out a relieved breath, and my pounding heart slowed to almost normal. They couldn't be after me. Probably didn't know I was here. I belly-scooted closer to the mine's entrance. What were they up to in the middle of the night?

From this distance, I only saw shadows. Scraping. Grunting. Several choice cuss words. After a few more minutes, a truck started. One man shouted, the others climbed in the back of the pickup, and they roared off across the desert.

I glanced at the moon overhead, and then the horizon. It would be light soon. I should check my treasure first and then see what was going on down below. I returned to the main cavern and flipped on my lamp. In the far left corner, I found the small petroglyph I'd scratched on the underside of a rock. My marker.

Crawling on hands and knees a hundred paces farther into the salt mine, I took the right fork when the tunnel split. Then a left, and another right. The cavern narrowed until I could hardly fit between the rough walls. I coughed, gagging on the dust.

Shouldn't stay too long. The air back here was stale. Dangerous. Moving the cairn of rocks, I checked my next plastic marker. I wiped the sticky sweat off my brow, and released a quick sigh. No one had disturbed the sacred site.

I reached down in the hole, and my fingers closed around the cool metal box. My shoulders sagged. Yes. Still there. A glint of silver flashed.

My treasure was safe.

# CHAPTER 10

Time to investigate the other mine. I replaced the box and moved toward the entrance. I took a long swig of tepid water, rinsed the salt and dust from my mouth and spit on a rock in the corner. Glancing around one more time, I made sure my emergency stash was well hidden. Then I crawled into the dawn.

From my high vantage point, nothing but empty desert surrounded me.

No truck.

No guys.

No one.

Half walking and half skidding, I slid down the steep hill to where the men had been working.

In the gully, tire marks still patterned the sand, only partially blown away by the early morning breeze.

A big truck. A few big footprints. Probably no big deal. Probably some small-time drug dealers using the place as a stash, but I'd better check.

Impatiently, I pulled away the rotted boards from the front of the smaller mine and crawled a few feet inside. Seemed bigger than last time I explored in here. And those were fresh timbers supporting the ceiling.

My heart stumbled, thudding erratically in my chest.

A shiny new iron gate blocked my way. I rattled the bars in frustration. No way was I getting through there. Rising up on my knees, I flashed my light into the corners of the tunnel. Damn. Nothing to see but salt-encrusted rock and a few old timbers. Had they emptied the place last night?

I sat on my haunches and rubbed my chin. Somebody was definitely using the mine as a hiding place. But who? And for what? The enormous gate was overkill if all they wanted to secure were a couple of bales of weed. Cocaine? It seemed weird they'd used an old mine with so many better places to hide dope.

I sucked in a few quick breaths, but my heart still pounded like powwow drums. Could it have anything to do with the grave robbers? Was the mine somehow connected to the tribe's stolen artifacts? And Morty's death?

I crawled into the fresh morning air and used a flat rock to pound the rotten boards into place. I needed to tell someone about the mine.

The big question was—who could I trust?

****

Later that morning, I juggled two hot drinks and knocked on the door at Angel's Cloud with the back of my heel. Backing up a few paces, I checked the open windows above. Forrest appeared between the lace curtains and waved.

A few minutes later, she quietly let herself out and sat down next to me on the tall curb near the street. After zipping her sweatshirt against the chilly morning, she accepted the drink with a quick nod and a smile. "When'd you get back?" Her voice barely rose above a whisper.

I glanced at the intense blue sky, the park across the street, the monster SUV full of tourists driving by.

"A few minutes ago. I had to check on stuff." I gave her a halfhearted shrug. It was the best truth I could give her right now.

Forrest shot me her pissed-off look again, and my cheeks heated even in the cold morning air.

She moved apart from me, her mouth downturned, her shoulders hunched away.

I wriggled under her stare. "It's better if you don't know everything. Safer."

She tossed her ponytail and took another sip. "Whatever."

Man. I felt like crap keeping secrets from her. I pushed my hair out of my eyes and resettled my body closer to hers.

She glared at me, and the green flecks in her eyes sparked with fury.

"Forrest. Come on."

"I understand, Josh. You don't trust me." Her chin tipped higher, and the little muscle in the side of her jaw flexed.

Totally pissed.

She glanced at me like I was a coyote turd. Worse, I felt like one. A low-down, lying coyote turd. Would she understand? And the even bigger question—did I have the guts to tell her who I really was? *What* I really was.

I touched her arm. "I'll tell you all about it…later."

She turned her head and finally met my gaze.

"Promise," I said, crisscrossing my chest with one finger. "Just not now, not here."

With a slight nod, she relaxed into her place and folded her hands around the cup, blowing on the liquid before sipping. "I have a new job."

I pulled back and shook my head in surprise. Girls switched gears so damn fast. I scratched the tip of my nose. At least she wasn't mad anymore.

She squared her shoulders and swayed back and forth in place like she was proud of herself. "The Connor Hotel needed someone to work weekends."

"When will we have time to investigate?"

"The job's only afternoons. A few hours a week. The hotel won't be busy until next month, when the snowbirds start showing up."

"I guess."

"An-n-nd since it's the only decent place in town. I'll get to snoop around all the visitors' rooms. Watch people coming and going." She waggled her eyebrows at me. "Maybe listen in a few doorways."

"Be careful, Forrest. Don't get caught."

"Ffft, nobody pays any attention to a teenage maid."

I smiled and relaxed my tense shoulders. "Sweet idea, Miss Scarlet. I'll help Rocky and Gina with bussing tables. Between the two of us, if something happens in town, we'll hear about it."

She jumped off the curb and recycled her cup with a self-satisfied grin. "Come on, Colonel Mustard. Let's go for a walk."

I followed her across the street, and we climbed, hand in hand, up the steep wooden stairs, where the tiny city park was squeezed between two tall retaining walls. The chains of an old swing set creaked in the morning breeze.

Forrest sat on the plank seat, tip-toed back, and then launched herself forward. She pumped her legs until she was swinging high above me. "Besides, Josh,

Gran and I need the money. I have to help her."

"I know. I get it."

She dragged her feet to slow the swing, and I stepped forward to grab both chains. A rush of blood warmed my face. Before I chickened out, I bent down and kissed her.

Her lips were cool from the morning, and sweet from the mocha.

Forrest slipped her arms around my waist, stroking my back even after I broke the kiss. I touched her cheek, and she smiled up into my face.

"Nice," she sighed, moving closer, as if for another taste. She kissed me this time, pulling me to her and wrapping her arms around my neck.

I could barely draw air. My whole body buzzed with an energy I'd never felt before. I wanted…

She stepped away. With a mischievous look in her smiling eyes, she pulled me toward the next flight of steps. "Race ya," she called over her shoulder with a bright laugh.

She was three steps ahead before I shouted, "No fair."

She beat me to the top. "I win. I get to ask you a question."

I raised one brow but didn't object. Was I puffing from taking the stairs three at a time, or the thought of kissing her again?

With both hands, she grabbed the front of my jacket. "What's your big secret?"

I put a dumb look on my face and frowned. Secret? Which one? I had too many.

She gave me a gentle shove. "Fair's fair. I've heard you have…talent."

"That's what people call it?"

"Well?"

I dodged her fierce gaze. "I'm good at algebra. In the advanced class," I said with bravado, but my stomach flipped over three times, like I'd done a full circle on those stupid swings.

"Spill it."

I turned away. "Don't, Forrest. Don't ruin it."

She caught me and put her face close to mine. "Nothing you could tell me will ruin anything." She said the words slowly, carefully, like she meant them.

"I've never told anyone."

"You can trust me."

"It's difficult to explain." I took her hand and walked toward the dilapidated Catholic Church perched at the top of the hill. I gave a quick wave to the old priest sunning himself on the steps.

"Is it because you're Native American?"

"Sorta. Hard to know. Not many Yavapai people can…" I stopped and stared at her. My stomach did another flip, and I swallowed the sour taste in the back of my throat. I glanced out over the barren desert landscape below us. A lonely cloud scuttled across the valley, trailed by its shadow.

How could I tell her how totally weird I really was? How would I even find the words?

If I counted the seconds until she turned and ran away from me, would that keep my heart from busting apart?

Would she still be standing there when I got to ten? Doubtful.

She waited for me, watching me with those beautiful, blue-green-waterfall eyes.

I swallowed the cholla bud spinning in my throat and began. "Sometimes things have a story, a history. I can touch things, and know about the story."

One.

Forrest worked her mouth, twisting one side and then the other. "What do you know?" Her tone sounded matter-of-fact, like she was asking a question in history class about the Battle of the Bulge.

Two.

"Depends. It's not like it's all important. Like where you got those little earrings."

She tossed her head, and the blue crystals sparkled in the light. "They're from Wal-Mart. Big deal."

Three.

I took her hand and rubbed my thumb over the soft skin on her palm. "Exactly, but some things are special. Or old. Or hold secrets about the people who've used them."

Little bumps scattered up her arms, but she didn't pull away. "You're giving me the shivers."

Four. Five.

I sat on an old bench, hunched over and folded my hands. "Sometimes it gives me the shivers, too. Or worse."

"Like the first day you came to my gran's store?"

I nodded.

"Like if you touched a gun, you could tell if it had killed someone?"

"Yes." I gave up on swallowing the cactus in my throat and stared out at the vast view of the canyons. A thousand feet below us, shadows of more dark clouds raced across the red mesas. The wind blowing up the mountain pushed Forrest's hair into her face. She tucked a strand behind her ear.

Six.

"Do you do it all the time? I mean, like, whatever you touch, you know its history?"

I shook my head. "Not now. When I was little, I couldn't control the…"

"Visions?"

I nodded. "But now I have a mentor. Norah, the lady I went to visit this summer in California, has been awesome."

"Norah?"

"Yes. She taught me to shield myself. To control the visions instead of letting them control me."

Forrest sat next to me on the bench and studied me for a long time. "I believe you."

My heart thumped, but in a good way.

Seven.

Like maybe she wouldn't laugh. Like maybe she really was my friend. Like maybe I could be happy. "Don't you want proof?"

She studied my face, her gaze moving from my lips to my eyes and back. "No."

I could barely breathe.

Eight. Nine.

She squeezed my hand lightly. "Can you read people the same way?"

"No."

Ten.

She stared out over the valley, too. "Then we make a pretty good team," she said more to herself than me.

"What's that mean?"

"Oh, no, Colonel Mustard." With a laugh, she started down the hill. "First you have to win a race."

# CHAPTER 11

*The following Monday after school*

I braced my foot on the school bleachers and tightened the laces of my track shoes. "Did you learn anything at the hotel yesterday?" I asked Forrest. I kept my voice low, hoping the rest of the cross-country team wouldn't hear.

Pulling her hair into a ponytail, Forrest twisted it together with a purple band. "I learned how to scrub toilets." She propped one foot on the bottom bench of the bleachers to stretch out her hamstrings before practice. "The place was almost empty because of the rain. Three cancellations." She leaned in closer to my ear. "How's George?"

"Supposed to get bailed out today."

"That's super great."

"Kwail," Coach Higgins shouted from across the playing field.

"Wait here. I'll see what he wants." I trotted over to the lanky man wearing grey sweats and a school mascot ball cap. "Yes, sir."

"Did you bring out the team roster from my office?"

I gave a quick groan. "Sorry, Coach. I forgot."

Coach Higgins gave a quick glance in Forrest's direction, and then said with a soft chuckle. "A little distracted these days, Kwail?"

My face heated. "I'll go get it for you now, sir."

I returned in a few minutes and grimaced. The team had left without me. My gut dropped and rolled around inside my running shoes. Even Forrest hadn't waited. I handed Coach the paperwork and dashed after the last stragglers.

I hadn't warmed up, so within ten minutes my muscles were cramping. At the top of a small rise, I limped to a stop and stretched out my hamstrings until the pain eased.

A half-dozen members of the cross-country team trotted in unison a quarter mile ahead, but I couldn't see Forrest's bright hair on the trail. My gut squeezed even tighter. Why hadn't she waited for me?

I skidded down the gravel hill and wind-sprinted the flat section of the run. I was puffing hard when I spotted her standing next to a couple tall saguaros on the next rise. I heard her voice and almost called out, but then a second voice spoke. A guy's.

A sick feeling launched into my throat. I ducked behind the tall clump of mesquite bushes, and a cold wave of nausea grabbed my gut. She was standing right next to that dumb-ass Dennis Robb.

Taking a silent step closer, I gritted my teeth until my jaw ached. I could see the two of them clearly, between the branches of the trees.

They could have seen me, too, if they'd been looking, but they were concentrating on each other. My nostrils flared as I sucked in a breath.

Forrest took a step closer to Dennis, smiling up into his idiotic face. She even twirled a lock of her hair with one finger as she chatted away.

Enough. I turned and ran back the way I'd come.

\*\*\*\*

After practice, Forrest stomped up the stairs of the bus and plopped down in the plastic seat next to me. "Where'd you run off to?"

I stared at the dirty rubber floor mat under my feet, pulse pounding through my body like a team of runners going downhill. If I said anything, I'd sound like a fool. Better to keep my great big jealous trap shut.

"Josh?" She huffed when I didn't answer. Crossing her arms, she waited.

I ignored my thumping heartbeats and her glare. I hated the silence.

"Fine," she hissed and gathered her books, as if she was going to leave.

"I tried to catch up. I wanted to talk to you, but you were having such a good time with Dennis…I didn't want to interrupt." Even though I worked to keep my voice steady, the last few words got away from me and rose to a ten-year-old's squeak. Stupid. I sounded so damn stupid. And jealous. Forrest would hate me.

She tipped her head to one side and studied my face for a long moment, then smiled with just the corners of her mouth. She leaned in. "I wanted to talk to Dennis to see if he knew anything about our…you know…our game of Clue. I thought, like…maybe his dad might let something drop at home."

I closed my eyes. What an idiot. An old-fashioned, slimy, algae-green-with-jealousy idiot. "Forrest, I…"

She laid one warm hand on my sleeve and kissed the side of my cheek. "You're so cute. You were jealous of Dennis Robb? Really?" She let out a pleased-sounding giggle, and then glanced around the bus to make sure no one was listening. Dennis hadn't boarded yet. "I can't stand that pompous, thinks-he-knows-everything showoff."

Relief flowed through me like cool water. "Sorry, I should have trusted you."

"Yes, you should have, but it's okay." She snuggled a little closer. "Did you find out anything at Rocky's over the weekend?"

I shook my head.

She let out a small huff through pursed lips. "We're totally awesome detectives, aren't we?"

I grunted.

"Well, we can drop Dennis from the list of suspects. He told me his dad took him to this fancy sports camp in Colorado for the whole month of August."

**\*\*\*\***

With a quick wave to Forrest, I jumped off the bus and headed down the two-block main street of Camp Verde. George should be home by now. Rocky and Gina had driven down from Jerome to post bail.

I quickened my footsteps, dodged between two parked trucks, and crossed the quiet street.

Bet George had some chili cooking, and I would help him get the Trading Post ready to reopen.

Whistling, I took the side street and loped up to the private entrance to the store. The door was unlocked, and I gave a happy whoop. "George?" I called through the kitchen.

Gina and Rocky got up from sitting at the table.

"Where's George?"

From the expression on Gina's face, I could tell the news wasn't good. "The judge denied his bail."

I dropped my pack with a thud. "What?" My gut

dropped to the floor too.

Rocky stepped closer. "George's tribal lawyer says there's quite a bit of evidence against him. Sheriff Robb spoke on George's behalf, but the DA and the judge wouldn't listen."

Gina patted my arm. Like that would help. "They transferred him to the county jail. He'll go before the grand jury soon."

"Then he can come home?"

She gave me another pained expression. "Doesn't look too good."

I wanted to kick a chair and launch it across the room, but nothing would ease my frustration. I leaned against the wall, blood pounding in my ears.

"We're so sorry, honey. We figured we'd wait to tell you until after practice."

"What do we do now?"

"He has a good lawyer," Rocky said. "We'll have to let this play out."

"Let him rot in jail?" I ground my teeth. "He's innocent."

"We know, dear." Gina gave a long sigh and came around to hug me. "Robb believes George is being framed, but the DA was adamant."

"You're welcome to stay with us," Rocky offered.

"I called Norah this afternoon," Gina continued. "She's worried about you, too. She invited you to come finish the school year in California. That might be better. Get you away from the Valley."

I shook the dizzy feeling out of my head. "No," I said too loudly, and then held up my hands. "Sorry. I'll stay with you, but what about the Trading Post?"

Rocky shrugged one of his big shoulders. "George

already told me to put the expensive pieces in the safe. Robb says he'll have a deputy drive by a couple of times a day. Place should be okay. For now."

"Go pack, Josh. It's a long drive up the hill," Gina said. "We'd better get started, or we'll never make Jerome before dark."

CHAPTER 12

"Josh, wait up," Forrest called. She bent over and grabbed her knees to catch her breath.

I trotted back down the path and handed her my water bottle.

She drank thirstily. "This is a steeper climb than I'm used to," she said when she recovered her normal voice. "Why are we taking the long way back to school?"

"I want to show you something. Coach won't mind." I took her hand and led her through a nearby break in the chain link fence.

Forrest glanced over her shoulder. "Are we supposed to be in here? Won't we get in trouble?"

I shrugged. We hiked uphill until we reached a maintained path. "I volunteered here last summer. The Ranger knows me, so he won't care if we go to the well."

"What is this place?"

"The United States government calls it 'Montezuma's Castle.'"

"The Cliff House? Gran brought me here when we first moved to Jerome."

"The Cliff House is part of the park. Of course, Montezuma never lived anywhere near here, but the name stuck, and it brings in the tourists traveling north to Flag."

We headed away from the low-slung buildings of the tourist center and up along a trail labeled Montezuma's Well.

"Not his either, I suppose," Forrest said.

"Nope."

We reached the edge of a small lake, and Forrest let out a sigh. "Pretty. Look how blue the water is."

I draped my arm on her shoulder. "Notice anything different about it?"

She stared at the pond. A light wind blew ripples across the rocks on the far side, igniting bright sparkles on her eyes. After a moment, she gave me a shrug. "I give."

"Here's a hint. Dragonflies."

She stared a little longer, her brows drawn down. "The water seems deep. Quiet."

"Yeah."

"Too quiet." She grabbed my arm. "There aren't any animals around. No fish in the shallows. No bugs. No birds."

"No dragonflies. The water's poison. It's full of arsenic."

"Who would do that?"

"It's natural. Always been that way. Even the ancient people knew the water was poison. Some scientists believe when the droughts came centuries ago, the people used the water despite the danger. That's why so many of them died."

I walked over and perched on top of a nearby picnic bench. A few tourists wandered down the path, but paid little attention to us.

I waved to the family and turned back to Forrest. "The park will close in a few minutes, but nobody will care if we stay."

I had something to say, something important. She seemed to understand, sitting quietly next to me until I was ready to continue. A cool breeze lifted her hair.

I tried to keep my face calm, but my pulse drummed rapidly on the side of my neck. I entwined my fingers with hers and closed my eyes. I couldn't look at her face right now. "My mother died when I was twelve."

Forrest squeezed my hand. "I'm sorry. Had she been sick?"

"She had diabetes for years, but it wasn't what killed her." I swallowed had to swallow hard before I could continue. "My uncle murdered her."

Forrest gasped. "I… Oh, my God, Josh. Why?"

"Mom was trying to protect me. She knew my secret."

"Your secret? About touching stuff and knowing its history?"

"No. Uncle Kenny knew that already. There was another, bigger secret. Mom knew I would have to find a treasure and return it." I spoke quietly, but my anger seethed behind my voice. "Uncle Kenny killed her for the clues to the treasure. He killed her and kidnapped me so I would help him."

"Holy crap."

"He gave her an overdose of insulin. The cops spent weeks figuring out she'd been murdered. Took them even longer to find me."

"Your Uncle Kenny had you all that time?"

I gave a slight nod. I didn't want to remember, but she needed to understand. "Yeah. At first I didn't know Kenny killed Mom. Not until I found the"—I swallowed past another lump—"the insulin needles."

Forrest covered my hand with hers. "How did you get away?" she asked in a tense whisper.

"Norah, my mentor, came after me. She talked a cop into helping her."

Forrest gulped, her face rigid, the skin around her mouth pale. Her hand felt cold in mine. I could tell she wanted to help, but there wasn't any way she could soothe me.

She closed her eyes, and so did I.

I pictured Uncle Kenny. A tall man. Huge. To me, anyway. With mean eyes and a cruel mouth. His darkness loomed over me, almost overwhelmed me. I had to block the pain and fear all over again.

I let go of her hand and stood, shaking off the cold. She didn't seem to notice. I focused on the ground, dragging a stick through the dust in a circular design I'd seen somewhere before.

Finally, I found enough air to continue. "For almost a year, I didn't understand why I ended up living with George."

"George adopted you."

"Yes, and he was great. Very patient." Remembering those first months, I had to laugh. "I was a real pain in the ass for a while. I was so angry."

"You were scared. Any kid would be."

I leaned back and stared at the sky. Closing my eyes to the golden light, I smiled. "Late at night, if I had a nightmare and couldn't sleep, George would tell me stories, legends about our people."

"I've read a few of those stories." Her mouth tilted up into a full smile. "I love the one about the coyote and the bird girls, but I did feel sorry for the poor little coyote when the birds took back all their feathers."

"The coyote often gets the worst of it, but most of the time he has it coming." I squinted to see her in the glare of sunlight. "You've read English translations of the stories. What I didn't realize at the time was George was telling me those tales in our language."

"Yavapai?"

"No. An even more ancient language. Many of the words date back to the Anasazi, the cliff dwellers. Some may be even older."

"Sick. But how did you understand?"

"When I was little, my mother told me the same stories. Somehow I understood, the same way I understand English. Now I know she spoke the language to me from the time I was born."

Forrest nodded and waited for me to continue.

"George told me the same stories over and over again. Exactly the same way, using the same words, even the same cadence, until I could repeat them myself, word for word."

"So totally awesome."

"It's part of my training."

She drew back her chin and blinked. "For what?"

"For when I become shaman for my tribe."

"Wicked, Josh. Like George is the medicine man?"

"Sort of. I'll help with the sick, too." I hitched one shoulder and then the other. "Sometimes I'll be more like an advisor. A keeper of the old ways. George says it's important, but I don't know. Most of the time it seems…" I glanced away and stared at the red-orange sunset in the distance.

"A little far-fetched?"

"Yeah. Like, unreal. How will I do anything

important for my tribe? I'm just a kid. An orphan. You know?"

\*\*\*\*

"Yeah." I knew. I closed my eyes, and the only memory I had of my mother flashed through my mind and then my heart. Turning my back to Josh, I bit my lip to keep back a cry of pain. My heart ached for him. And for myself.

"An orphan," I said to the wind. "Like me."

# CHAPTER 13

*Later that week*

I hefted the rack of dirty glasses and leaned against the swinging kitchen door. The late-night crowd at Rocky's Roost had thinned out early, and most of the bikers were already headed home. Supposed to rain soon. The band from the Haunted Hamburger would need another round, but Gina needed to serve the beer.

A jacked guy stepped in through the open door and glanced around the bar. Rough clothes, long hair, mean eyes.

I frowned. Transient.

The guy stopped and straightened his shoulders. Gina could usually handle anyone who walked into the bar, but this guy was trouble. She glanced up and stilled.

When the man approached her, he pulled off the worn brown hat speckled with rain and clutched it to his chest. He licked his lips and cast his dark, almond-shaped eyes in the direction of his worn boots.

I squinted and angled my head to get a different perspective. Something didn't fit. I set down the glasses and stayed put.

The guy had been on the road for a while. His clothes and backpack were the color of dirt. His dark hair was matted and dirty, pulled back from his face in a greasy tail, but his eyes were sharp and took in everything in his surroundings—every expression, every move, every bottle and glass.

With one hand on her hip, Gina cleared her throat and gave him her don't-eff-with-me-look. "We're closin' soon."

The man leaned one elbow on the bar. When he smiled, the crinkles around his eyes moved in unison. "Got anything a hungry guy could eat?"

Rocky pushed through the swinging door from the kitchen. "Hey, Manny. How's it goin'?" He clasped hands with the guy. "You're hungry? Josh, get that turkey sandwich out of the fridge. The one Gina made by mistake."

I sighed, turned, and did as I was told. Damn. I had plans for that turkey sandwich. When I returned from the kitchen, Rocky had served the guy a beer and they were face-to-face, chuckling at some corny joke Rocky must have told.

The man scratched his week-old scruff, and I felt itchy, but I handed over the sandwich. The expression on Manny's face was almost friendly. Almost.

The guy wolfed the sandwich in three bites and wiped his mouth with the back of his hand. "I'm pretty tired. Been traveling south for three days. There a place around here I could stay for the night?"

Rocky thumbed over his shoulder. "Lean-to around the corner. Cot and a blanket. Not much, but it's dry."

"Thanks, man. More than I usually get." Manny drained his beer and headed for the side door. "I can do a few chores in the morning to pay ya back."

\*\*\*\*

Saturday morning came early. Rocky's big boots clumped across the living room floor, and the whole house shook.

With a low groan, I turned on my side and squinted at the pale light coming through my window. I pulled the covers over my face. Time to get up already?

A big hand knocked on the door. "You helping out this morning?"

"Yeah." I pushed back the blanket and put my feet on the cold floor. Blurry-eyed, I shuffled into the kitchen.

Rocky put two cups of coffee on the counter. "Take this to the traveler. Tell him there's a stack of logs to chop right outside the door to the shed, if he's good for his word."

"He's probably already gone." Back in my room, I tugged on my jeans, shoes and hoodie. Cups in hand, I went out the back way and squinted at the bright desert light. The whack of an axe came from around the corner.

Manny had stripped to a filthy T-shirt. A half cord of wood stood chopped and stacked against the wall. His huge shoulders steamed in the cold morning air.

I smiled into my mug. Maybe the guy was okay.

He accepted the cup and slurped the hot liquid. "Man, that's good. Your dad's cool."

"Not my dad."

"No?"

"Sorta my uncle."

Manny grunted and put down the coffee on a nearby stump. He positioned his feet and chopped another log in one swift blow. Guy was ripped.

Curious, I leaned against the rough wooden shed and studied the stranger. He was scruffy enough to be a transient, but now I'd observed him, there were a couple of details that didn't fit.

His nails were dirty, but they were all trimmed short, not broken. Manny smiled over at me while he stacked another huge log. His teeth were even and white and clean.

"Figured it out already?" Manny put down the ax and fisted one hand on his hip.

"Undercover cop?"

"Rocky said you were smart."

"Why're you here?"

"To help you."

I sloshed my coffee and burned my fingers. With a hiss, I set down the cup. "You mean help George?"

"Him too."

"Who told you?"

"Don't worry about that."

"Let me hold your shield."

Manny's eyes opened wider, but then he chuckled and dug down to the bottom of his pack. He handed over the silver badge hidden in a leather case.

Cautiously, I opened my senses, and it only took a second to know what I needed to know. Guy was for real. I let out a long breath and handed Manny back his ID. "George didn't kill Marty."

"Yeah. Figured that."

"Then get him out of jail. He's been stuck behind bars for more than a week now. Nobody's doing anything."

"He's better off there right now. We might need to get you somewhere safe, too."

My heart started to race, and I backed up a half a step. "I don't get it."

"Josh? You there?" Forrest called from around the

corner.

Manny picked up the ax. "Don't say anything about who I really am."

I nodded. He whacked another log. "I'll be in touch."

Quickly, I ducked around the building and called, "Hey."

Forrest crossed the street and joined us. She frowned briefly at the man, but took my hand. "What's up?"

"Forrest, meet Manny."

"Don't," Manny growled under his breath. His expression changed as he took on the character of a transient again. Sharper, meaner, more threatening.

She studied the man carefully. "Who's he?"

"Told you…"

I pulled my shoulders back and stuck out my chin. "She's in on the whole thing. If you want to talk to me, she can listen. I trust her."

The man's gaze travelled up, then down, but his expression remained hostile.

"Cop?" she asked matter-of-factly.

Manny rubbed the back of his neck. "Didn't say…"

"Didn't have to," she replied with some extra sass in her tone. She took a step closer and hiked up her chin.

I chuckled to myself. Man, she was so cool. I put an arm around her shoulder and squeezed. Even with George in jail, I felt a sudden…happiness. I smiled into her pretty eyes, and my heart did cartwheels.

## CHAPTER 14

*Sunday afternoon*

"Park the jeep behind the gas station." I pointed to the highway off-ramp and braced for Forrest's quick reaction.

She floored the gas pedal and swung the steering wheel to the right, dodging the oncoming traffic.

Somehow I'd survived the drive down the mountain. I closed my eyes a few times, but Forrest hadn't killed us. I smiled up into the intense blue of the sky and gave thanks.

It was a risk, a big risk, but letting her drive was the only way we'd have time to check out the mines. There were things I still needed to explain, and my hideout was the perfect place to finally tell Forrest the truth, ghost and all.

Glad to be on solid ground, I jumped out of the jeep and grabbed my pack from the rear seat. "Now we walk."

"How far?" she asked, matching my pace.

"Couple miles."

"Tilley can four-wheel. Why not drive all the way?"

"Better chance we won't be seen. Your jeep is a little…"

"Obvious?" she finished my sentence. She shrugged and hiked in silence beside me. The dirt road was silent.

The sun felt warm against my shoulders, but the summer heat had left the desert. Fall was my favorite time of year. Migrating birds were returning, and soon the desert would green with winter rains.

After walking down the road a few miles with no one passing us, I finally relaxed. "Cutting over this rise will save us some time." I held up the top line of a rusty barbed wire fence. Forrest climbed between the sharp strands.

We set off cross-country. The saguaros guarding the high ground gave way to spear-tipped agave.

"Watch the cholla." I took her hand and led her around the prickly jumping cactus.

The trail, no more than a deer track, wound down into a wide arroyo. We crossed the crunchy dirt of the dry river bed and climbed the far side. Few cacti grew this close to the mine.

"Stay here," I said, and she nodded without comment.

I climbed the rest of the way up the hill and peeked over the ridge between an outcropping of boulders. My shoulders relaxed. My breath came easier. The mines were deserted.

I waved to Forrest, and she climbed the embankment. We slid down the salt-encrusted gravel to the abandoned mines below.

She glanced around the rocky outcropping. "What is this place?"

"It's an ancient salt mine. My ancestors dug and traded salt."

"Like, in the last century?"

With a grunt, I pulled away the timbers and

checked my marker. "Like eight hundred or maybe a thousand years ago."

She leaned down to peek into the dark cavern, and her eyes widened.

I searched in my pack and handed her a headlamp, then strapped another one on my forehead.

She licked her lips and frowned. "We're going in there?" She squeaked out the last word.

"Do it all the time."

"I don't like dark places." She backed up a step and handed me the light. Her face had gone very pale. "How 'bout I play lookout?"

I took her hand. "It's safe. I've shored up the cave-ins."

She took two more steps back. "You're totally not convincing me."

"We'll go into the first part, okay? The cavern's only a few feet from here. It's a big room. You can stand up."

She shook her head, terror flickering over her face.

I let out a sigh. "Okay, I'll go first. Put on some lights. Get it all ready so it's not scary."

Her brows cut worry lines into her forehead. "Maybe."

I gave her a quick squeeze and crawled through the narrow opening.

****

I mangled my lip and counted to twenty, again.

Pacing in front of the entrance of the stupid salt mine, my arms clutched to my chest to keep from trembling. "Josh?" I called into the terrifying black hole.

Ten minutes had passed since he disappeared down

that dark pit. My heart was pounding even harder than before, and I chewed my last long fingernail until it started to bleed.

"Josh," I shouted again, and my voice came back in ominous echoes. Now my heart was really going. I felt a little dizzy and dropped to my knees. Was he in trouble?

I clamped on the headlamp and brushed away the sweat stinging my eyes. Was he hurt? Trapped? Would I have to go in that…that awful place and find him?

I lay down on my belly and pulled myself a few feet into the dark, but then I heard his shout.

"Hang on, Forrest. I'm coming out."

Gratefully, I reversed direction and backed out as fast as I could.

When Josh appeared at the entrance, covered with dust, I grabbed him and kissed him. Hard. He tasted like salt. And dirt. And sweat. I checked him all over, like my grandmother checked me when I fell down the stairs.

"I'm fine," he laughed. "Were you worried?"

I nodded and took three deep breaths to slow my pulse.

"Come on." He crawled back in.

"Heck." I followed. I closed my eyes. There was nothing to see anyway. I kept one hand on his ankle and belly-scooted forward. I smelled salt, tasted it. Even with my lids closed, the corners of my eyes stung.

"Open your eyes, Forrest."

I pulled up on my knees and reached over my head. I couldn't touch the rocky ceiling anymore. I opened my eyes and sucked in a sharp breath. "Beautiful."

Josh had placed a few battery-powered electric

lanterns around the cave. The space was the size of my bedroom, and every surface was covered with tiny, glistening crystals.

I stood and touched the wall. "It's like being inside a geode."

Grinning, Josh crossed his legs and sat by the far wall. He offered me a bottle of water, and I drank thirstily.

Knees to knees, I sat close enough to touch him and studied his face. "Why do you come here?"

"It's sacred."

Suddenly, his attention shot to the far wall, and he drew in a harsh breath. His gaze was unfocused, and his smile slacked to nothing.

"What?" As I turned, a cold chill brushed across my face.

Josh didn't respond.

"Josh?" I took his arm, gently at first, but then with more force. "Josh, you're freaking me out."

He took my hand, but kept his gaze in the distance. Then he nodded. "Yes. I know."

"Know what?" I hissed, rubbing the goose bumps on my arms. "Who…?"

"But how?" he asked over my question.

I swallowed hard. His voice sounded way different. Breathless.

Haunted.

My heart slammed against my ribs. Time to bug out.

Then, just as suddenly as he'd disappeared, the real Josh was back. He smiled and brushed the tears from the corners of my eyes. "I need to go get something. It'll only take a minute."

I shook her head once and grabbed him by the shoulder. "Don't leave me here alone. Or worse."

"You can follow me down into the mine, but the tunnel is long, and low, and very narrow."

"No way."

He took my hands and rubbed them until they were warm again. "I promise. Nothing…no one…will hurt you."

I nodded, but glanced around the cavern. "Are we alone now?"

He smiled. "For the moment. Did you see him?"

"No, but I knew someone was here. You got this totally psycho look on your face."

"I'll explain everything in a minute." He gave me a quick, salty kiss and disappeared down a black tunnel.

"Promise?" I called after him.

His happy laugh echoed through the cavern.

I curled into a tight ball and waited in the light, concentrating on the reflections of the crystals on the ceiling and chewing on my last nail.

\*\*\*\*

I dug up the treasure in no time. Then I squeezed through the last narrow place and crawled into the lighted cavern, holding the cat necklace in my hand.

Head down, Forrest huddled in the corner, hugging her knees and rocking.

Poor kid. My mouth twitched. She hated being inside the mine, but she waited, just like she promised. I glanced over and gave a quick nod to the Magician.

I put an arm around her and rubbed her shoulder gently. "You managed to stay by yourself."

She was trembling and leaned into me. "Barely. Another minute and I would have booked it for sure."

I hesitated, my stomach roiling like a cement mixer. "I wanted to show you this." I held out the sacred necklace, and the silver glinted in the light.

"Wow," she breathed. "Where'd you get that?"

"It was a present. Sort of. A couple of years ago, I did a favor for someone special, and he gave me this in return. It's very old."

I laid the cat necklace on her outstretched palms, and she held it up next to the lantern. "Beautiful."

I needed to tell her about the Magician, but she was already scared shitless. Would she run away screaming if I started talking about ancient ghosts? I looked away…at the crystals, at my feet. Or would she laugh and tell everyone I was a freak?

She touched the necklace, drawing her fingertips across the intricately set turquoise and coral mosaic of a saber-toothed cat. She glanced up at me, and her hand gently touched my chest.

Warmth.

I trusted her.

"Is it from the ghost?"

My brows shot up. "Yes."

Funny. Her tone sounded calm, almost matter-of-fact.

"I won't laugh, Josh. I promise."

\*\*\*\*

Forrest nibbled the last cookie.

She appeared calm enough, considering she was sitting three feet from a ghost she couldn't see.

She glanced over at me. "What does it feel like to be haunted?"

I rubbed my mouth with the back of my hand. "He's not scary, if that's what you mean. He doesn't pop up and shout 'Boo!' in the middle of the night."

"Hope not." She shivered and leaned against me. "But I mean…do you feel special?"

I scooted back against the cave wall, and held her next to me. "I guess I never thought of it that way." I shrugged one shoulder and fiddled with the water bottle, tipping it over and then righting it.

The gravel scritched against her boot when she moved even closer. "You are special."

"Hardly."

"You said you'll be your tribe's shaman one day."

I glanced up. "When I'm grown…when I'm ready. Probably years from now."

I set down the bottle. "Someday I'll help lead the tribe. My father would have, if he'd lived, but first I must earn my place. I still have tons to learn."

She rose up on her knees and faced me. "Will you have magical powers?"

I laughed and pushed her playfully. "No. Mostly I'll sit in council meetings and decide lame stuff like where to put the medical clinic, or how much to spend on field trips for the schoolkids."

She aimed her headlamp into my eyes. I squinted, but held still while she studied me. "No. There's more to it."

"What do you mean?"

"This ghost of yours. He was someone special."

"I suppose."

"Tell me about him." She said the words in such a matter-of-fact way that I finally had the courage.

"I call him the Magician."

"And he lived a long time ago?"

I nodded. "When he died, he was buried with great

honor. He was hidden in a sacred place, but even then his grave was robbed."

"How did you help him?"

"I returned his tools. The ones his apprentice had stolen."

"A grave robber? That many centuries ago?"

I gave a quick nod. "George told me the legend. Some time after the Magician died, the apprentice stole the artifacts from the grave. A water bowl. A tiny seed basket. Some…other stuff. Stupid guy thought he would help the tribe if…"

"…if only he had the magic tools," Forrest finished for me.

"The apprentice was killed soon after he ransacked to the grave, and the tools were lost for centuries."

"How'd the apprentice die?" Forrest asked in a hushed whisper.

I swallowed hard. "He fell off a cliff."

"Wow."

"It gets even spookier. Remember I told you about Uncle Kenny?"

She nodded. Her eyes wide, she watched me carefully. "The creep who kidnapped you to get a treasure?" Her eyes widened, and she looked down at the necklace. "This treasure?"

"This was part of it."

"What happened?"

"Kenny fell off a cliff, too. I'm pretty sure the Magician sorta… pushed him."

She gave a long, low whistle. "Like, major irony."

# CHAPTER 15

I raised my hand toward Josh, and the knowledge washed into my mind. A cold shiver zinged down my neck and across my shoulders. "You returned the Magician's tools. You went into his burial site."

He nodded. "Norah, my friend, helped me. By that point she could see the ghost too. She told me what to do."

The goose bumps returned, big time, racing up and down my arms like Popsicle ants. "But you kept the necklace."

"Not exactly. The Magician returned it to me. Later…"

Time stopped. My breath suspended. In a split second, the vision came into sharp focus in my mind.

*The ghost, a tall man with long, black hair. An ancient city built in the walls of a red rock canyon.*

"A flute," Josh added, his voice barely audible, even in the heavy quiet of the mine.

I forced my consciousness back to him. "The little one? What's so special about the flute?"

Josh blushed a deep, ruddy color under his bronze skin. He jumped up and dusted off his jeans. "We better get moving. It'll be sunset in an hour, and we need to get back to the jeep."

Damn it. He avoided the question neatly.

Interesting. What was it about the flute that caused him so much embarrassment?

"Sure," I replied, waiting for the truth to come to me, but he was moving too quickly toward the opening of the cave for me to retrieve the impressions I'd seen a moment ago. I needed to understand and hurried after him.

He took my hand. "Want me to go first?"

"Josh, wait." I moved up close and touched his chest lightly with my palm. My power sizzled through my fingertips, but before I could see anything, Josh grabbed my wrist.

"What are you doing?" His voice sounded sharp, and echoed in the small space.

"Nothing." I dropped her hand behind my back.

"That's a lie." The words hissed out between his clenched teeth.

"Can we get out of here first?" I said. "Then I'll explain."

\*\*\*\*

Boy, was Josh pissed. He stomped down the sandy trail ahead of me, his footprints leaving potholes of fury in the grit. He held his shoulders, his neck, his hands stiffly. Resistant to my thoughts.

"My turn?" I called ahead.

Whirling around, Josh crossed his arms and let out a snort.

I caught up with him. "I kinda know stuff, too."

He glared at me. His eyes were muddy brown instead of the soft amber I loved.

I dropped my gaze and toed the sand with my hiking boot. "Sometimes I can tell stuff about people."

With another angry breath, he said, "Like what?"

"Just stuff." I hesitated, hitching one arm and then the other behind my back. "I can't do it all the time, or with everyone. Some people are more…tuned-in than others."

"You read minds?"

"No, not exactly." I fingered my dangling earring. "It's like you said. Some things aren't important. Like where I got these." I took his wrist, turned it over and dropped the silver wire and blue beads into his palm.

He closed his eyes. "Wal-Mart. $3.95. Marked down from $8.99. Plus tax. The cashier had red hair and a nose ring."

My heart ka-thumped in my chest. "Wicked."

He watched me through the narrow slits of his eyelids. "None of that's important."

"Exactly, but the fact that she hasn't told anyone her jerk-of-a-boyfriend abuses her might be."

Still frowning, he turned and hurried down the trail, striding along at a furious pace. I followed. After a few moments of uncomfortable static, I continued, breathless. "When I was little, I didn't understand I could do something special."

"You thought everyone knew what other people were thinking?"

"It's not like I hear words inside my head. Or voices. I'm not crazy. It's more a feeling, or a picture of someone's thoughts."

"What about my thoughts? Can you picture them?"

I dropped my chin and let my hair fall over my face. "Sometimes, but not now. I block them most of the time."

We stood at a high point of the hill, and he stared out over the desert landscape. The sun rested on the top of the high mountains to the west, and the clouds were backlit with vivid color.

"I try not to intrude. It isn't fair. When I was a kid, the visions were overpowering at times. I didn't understand. Couldn't explain. I just didn't have the words. When I came to live with Gran, I think she thought I'd gone a little daft. I always knew what was for dinner before she even went to the kitchen."

Josh started hiking again, but I knew he was listening.

My heartbeat stopped zig-zagging and slowed to almost normal. I dropped into step next to him, and he shortened his stride.

"Then when I was about seven, my Aunt Lilly, my mother's sister, took me to the beach one day. We went for a long walk, just the two of us. She explained what was going on in my head."

He leaned closer, like he was totally hearing me now.

"She taught me to shield the thoughts I didn't want to hear. It took some time, lots of practice, but I'm pretty good at it now."

"When you touched my chest back in the cave, it was like a bolt of energy zapped me. Then I felt your shield drop," Josh said.

Eyebrows raised, I glanced at him. "No one ever noticed before."

He shrugged. "Can you read lies?"

"Oh, yeah." I tucked my thumbs under the straps of my pack. The uphill hike had me breathless again, but soon my body relaxed into the pace. "That's the easiest part. The pictures don't match the words. Sometimes the visions are dark, full of shadows, like the truth is smeared with lies."

When we reached the jeep, I dug in my jeans pocket for my keys. Josh climbed in beside me.

I sucked in air, but instead of looking at him, I watched the changing hues of purple and orange clouds on the western skyline. A few lights, the lights from Jerome, twinkled near the top of the mountain. "My mom had the same gift, if that's what you want to call it, but it got her into trouble. Big trouble. I mean, that's why she's…gone."

I heard his intake of breath, but he continued to stare at the sunset with me, waiting. Should I tell him more? No. I'd been warned too many times. Telling would get more people killed.

I poked the key into the ignition with more force than necessary, and Tilley ground to a start. Change the subject. "Are you mad I didn't tell you before?"

Josh blew out a small puff of air, and one side of his mouth dipped into a frown. "I wish you'd been honest with me."

"I didn't lie, but it's true I didn't tell you everything." Toe on the clutch, I put Tilley in gear and waited.

He leaned his head on the headrest and entwined his fingers with mine. "I guess holding hands with my own personal lie detector won't hurt our investigation, Miss Scarlet."

\*\*\*\*

The drive home wasn't too scary. Forrest seemed consumed with her thoughts, and took the ragged curves at an almost-survivable speed.

On the one straight section of road, I glanced at the stern expression on her face. Her mother was gone.

What did that mean? Gone? Was she dead? Or living in a shack in South America?

As we squealed around the last curve into town, I studied her again and almost asked my question.

No. The set of her shoulders spoke clearly. She wasn't ready to divulge her secret. I'd have to wait.

Since it was the weekend, and the town was filled with snowbirds, we drove around ten minutes to find a parking place. Finally she managed to nab a spot in the narrow alley behind Rocky's bar.

Long purple shadows stretched out from the mesas onto the desert floor below us. A quarter-moon lit one corner of the sky. She turned in her seat to face me. "I'll ping you."

I shook my head. "We shouldn't text anymore."

Forrest pulled back, and her brows dropped as she studied my expression.

"No texts, no email, no nothing," I said, lowering my voice, even though there was no one nearby.

"You think this is big, don't you?" Her whisper matched mine in decibels and intensity.

"We don't want anyone to know what we're doing. And we don't want to leave any kind of trail."

"So we shouldn't talk on the phone, either."

"Right. At least not about the case."

She reached over, and with two fingers brushed the hair out of my eyes. "Be careful."

She kissed me. Soft. Sweet.

Then again. This one hot. My body buzzed with energy.

I reached for her and pulled her to me, needing to feel her warmth. When I skimmed my hand down her hair, Forrest shivered under my touch.

She pulled back, and I was afraid to speak. My voice would sound like some dorky sixth grader again.

With a smile, she left me alone in the jeep, and for a long time I stared at the moon. A flow of voices floated down from somewhere above me.

A woman laughed. Music.

I closed up the jeep and floated in through the back door of the bar.

## CHAPTER 16

*The next Friday afternoon*

"Where'd you learn to fix cars?" I asked.

Forrest glanced up from under the hood of her jeep and gave me what looked like a nostalgic smile. "A neighbor taught me," she said. "Several years ago, when we were still living in Pescadero, Gran and I would go next door, and I'd help this old guy named Malcolm work on his '52 sports car. He and Gran were 'friends.'" She air-quoted the last word.

"Sweet."

"Where'd you learn?"

"Mostly from George." I handed her the socket wrench she'd need to pull the last spark plug. "He had an old Buick we kept running. Got three hundred thousand miles out of it before a drunk stole it one night and smashed it up."

"Grrr. This one's stuck." Forrest leaned into the job and muscled the last one loose. "There." She held out the greasy plug with a satisfied grin on her dirt-smudged face.

"Nicely done, Miss Scarlet. Want me to adjust the gap while you clean up?"

"Sure."

"There're some rags over by my pack. And some Goop."

She helped herself while I gapped the plug. "This

should help the backfire, but we still need to check the transmission."

"I put in some fluid last week, but I think it's still leaking."

"Probably needs a gasket," I said while gapping the plugs. "It's a major job. Maybe Rocky can help us next weekend."

When she didn't answer, I glanced over toward where she stood. She was staring at me in a funny way, and sudden tension gripped my shoulders. My neck. My heart. "What?" I asked. "Did I say something wrong?

She beamed at me and laughed a short, happy-sounding laugh. "You're so great, Josh."

"Well, I know that." I gave a humble shrug. "You've just noticed?"

She gave me a playful, you-get-what-I-mean shove. "Here we are, hanging out, fixing Tilley like we're a couple of guys."

"You, Ms. Forrest Morgan, are no guy." I gave her an eyebrow waggle, and she laughed again.

She stomped her foot. "No. It's nice not to have to pretend. I can do whatever I feel like with you, like fix my car. I don't have to impress you. I don't have to giggle and curl my hair if I don't feel like it."

"Or put on makeup?"

"Yeah. Or put on makeup."

I smiled and put down my wrench. "I like you, too. Wanna go on a real date?"

She blinked three times. "Sure."

"I've saved up some money working nights at Rocky's. I need to go visit George in the morning, but why don't we go have dinner at the Haunted Hamburger tomorrow night? My treat."

She seemed to be thinking for a minute. The pink in her cheeks flashed a little pinker. "Tomorrow night?"

"Do you like cheesecake?"

"Totally adore it."

\*\*\*\*

I knocked on the door to Angel's Cloud and yanked my new tie back and forth a few times. Feeling itchy, I tugged my jacket closed and buttoned it. Then unbuttoned it. Gina insisted I needed new clothes for my "big date." She'd dragged me to the mall near Prescott to try on stuff.

I inspected myself in the reflection on front window and had to smile. Blue shirt. Tan jacket. Snazzy tie I picked out myself. I even had new shoes. The shiny leather kind.

Not half bad. A haircut let my ears show, and I was surprised to see they didn't stick out as much as they used to.

When I heard footsteps inside the shop, my heart thumped.

High-heeled footsteps. My stomach dropped.

Forrest opened the door, and I held on to my chin so it didn't hit the doorstep.

Wow. She looked smokin' hot. Her summer dress was just short enough to show off her great, long legs. The color did something to her eyes that made me a little dizzy. Her hair was pulled into a long ponytail with shiny blue ribbons holding it together. Man, I wanted to pull those ribbons.

"Isn't she pretty?" Angel Wings cooed from beside her.

"Gran!"

"Well, you are," the woman insisted. "Do you want

to come in, Josh?"

Forrest did a dramatic eye roll just for me. "No, we better go now, Gran. We'll be home later." Forrest gave her a quick kiss, came outside, and pulled me away from the shop entrance.

"She talked me into this dress at the store today." Forrest glanced down at the soft blue material.

"You're beautiful."

She stopped and inspected my face, then smiled her open, all-teeth-and-happiness-smile. "Thanks. You look pretty hot yourself. Come on. I'm starving."

****

"Hey there, Forrest." An effeminate waiter glided over to our table in the busy restaurant. With thinning blond hair and a paunch, he flipped his hand to his hip and grinned. "So, cutie, have you come for your weekly slice of chocolate cheesecake?"

Blushing, I shushed him with a finger to my lips.

Josh chuckled. "You are so busted."

The waiter put his hand over his mouth. "Oh sorry, sweetie. Was that our special little secret?"

"Not anymore." I sighed. "Josh. This is Ronald. When we moved into the shop, he helped Gran with the plumbing. He calls himself The Fixit Fairy."

Josh gave Ronald a friendly nod.

I cleared my throat and tried to lead the conversation away from my guilty pleasure. "So, Ronald, is your band playing tonight?"

"In just a few. We're so-o-o busy this weekend, so I'm filling in for one of the waitresses. Her kid's sick."

I turned back to Josh. "Ronald plays a mean sax in his jazz band."

"Awesome."

"So, sweetie." The waiter gave Josh a none-too-subtle once-over. "Is this hunk yours, or is he on the market?"

I laughed. "Hands off, Ronnie. He's mine."

Josh glanced at me and grinned.

Ronald brushed a hand over his carefully groomed hair and pretended to pout. "Too young for me, anyway."

I giggled.

"Here, Josh." He pulled a card from his apron pocket with a flourish. "If you need a handyman, I'm your guy. Fixit-Fairy to the rescue. Like the card says."

After we ordered our cheeseburgers and extra-crispy fries, Ronald hustled off to the kitchen.

"He's a big tease," I began moving my silverware back and forth in front of me, hoping my voice sounded normal. Yeah, right. Hoping the dim lighting in the restaurant hid my bright pink cheeks? It probably didn't.

Josh leaned forward and took my hand in his. "I don't mind being claimed," he said under his breath.

He squeezed my fingers gently, and my heart did a loop-the-loop. Then I looked across the crowded room, and it crash landed. "Oh, shit."

Near the entrance of the busy restaurant, Dennis Robb stood in line at the to-go desk.

Josh turned around and then quickly turned back.

"Put your head down. Maybe he won't see us," I hissed.

Josh clenched his fists on the table.

I grimaced, and every muscle in my body went tense. "He's coming this way. Please, Josh. Don't make a scene."

Funny, but Dennis had an almost sheepish expression on his face as he approached. Not his usual cocky, I-rule-the-world swagger. "S'up, Forrest?"

Josh roughly pushed back his chair and was standing like some fighter on one of those stupid wrestling shows. Then I saw the bruises around Dennis's eye.

Dennis put up his hands, palms out. "Listen, man, don't want no trouble. I came to say I'm sorry."

"For what?" Josh ground out, but I heard the surprise in his voice.

"About George."

"He's innocent."

"Course. He's cool. George was always great to me. He couldn't hurt nobody."

Josh dropped his hands and relaxed his stance.

"Oh and…" Dennis continued. "Sorry for hassling you, Forrest, the other day in the quad."

"That's okay, Dennis," I said quickly. "No prob."

Would the creep go away now?

"Yeah, well." The boy dropped his chin and turned to leave. "Later." He headed over to the take-out window, grabbed a brown bag of food, and took off out the door.

"Man," Josh blew out a quick breath.

I leaned back in my chair and brushed the hair out of my eyes. "I thought for a second there I was going to have to tear you two testosterone-driven bulls apart."

Josh shot me a what-are-you-talking-about face and pulled out his seat to sit down. "That was weird."

I chewed on the inside of my lip for a moment. "Josh, did you see his shiner?"

"Yeah. Up close, you could tell he'd been slugged

a couple times."

"But who? He's the biggest bully around."

"Not anymore."

CHAPTER 17

"I'm so full." I groaned and flopped down on the couch in Gina's front room.

Josh chuckled and sat down beside me. "You shouldn't have eaten the rest of my chocolate lava cake."

"Leaving even a bite of the dessert would have been a sin." I pointed a finger in his direction. "I don't get desserts like that. Ever."

He shot me a don't-fib-to-me squint.

"Well, almost never."

Josh rose and headed for the door leading up to the bar. "I'm going to check in and see if Gina needs me tonight for cleanup. Turn on some music if you want. Rocky's old stereo looks like a seventies' dinosaur, but the sound's primo."

The door slammed behind him, and I stretched to enjoy the quiet for a moment, then got up and ambled over to look out the window at the view below. Across the dark desert, lights from Camp Verde glowed in the distance, and a sliver of moon hung in the clear night sky. I smiled at my reflection in the window glass.

I did a little dance and happily hugged myself. Our first real date had rocked.

Maybe Josh would kiss me again tonight. Maybe he'd kiss me more than once. I let out a long, dramatic sigh, like girls did in the movies when they'd just noticed a hunky guy. Josh kissed nice. Awesome, in fact. I felt totally tingly when he even got close to me.

I wandered over to the mismatched collection of bookcases on the far wall. Rocky's stack of old vinyl records was a whole lot like the one Gran owned. I flipped through the funny, square albums. Stones, Led Zeppelin…and Neil Diamond? I wrinkled my nose. That couldn't be Rocky's.

I dug around and found an old Eagles record, put it on the turntable, and turned the volume down low. "Take it e-e-easy," crooned Glenn Fry. I turned over the album cover. The guy was totally hot way back then.

Inspecting the bookcase, I found mostly romance novels and submarine stories. The bottom shelf held textbooks and a copy of Moby Dick. I flipped through the beat-up, secondhand book and noticed a bookmark near the very end. Wow. Had Josh read the whole thing?

When I pushed the book back onto the shelf, the tiny flute I'd seen at the Trading Post rolled out. He'd hidden it behind his chemistry textbook.

I glanced behind me to make sure no one was looking, and picked up the wooden instrument. I drew my fingers along the finely inlaid decoration around the top. Pretty. Little turquoise and coral squares made a pattern of swirls and small birds.

I used to play the recorder back in grade school. This had to be pretty much the same. I covered the holes down the front with my fingers, brought the flute to my mouth and blew.

The music should come out the bottom, but all I managed was an airy whistle. The harder I blew, the more piercing the screech became. Finally one squeak and a couple almost clear notes.

"You know what it's used for, don't you?" Josh said.

Turning, I hid the flute behind me, and felt my cheeks burn.

"Sorry. I didn't mean to snoop. It…"

"It's okay, Forrest. You can't hurt it."

I dropped my hands to my sides and smiled. "It's pretty." I moved toward him and handed him the flute. "I saw you play it before at the Trading Post, and I wanted to give it a try."

When Josh put the instrument to his mouth, lilting music filled the room.

It wasn't loud, and the melody was simple, but the notes flowed around me. "Mmm. Nice. The sound's so pure, the music almost tickles me."

Josh put aside the flute and focused his gaze on me. The soft, amber color of his irises darkened to pure gold. He smiled and kissed me gently, drawing his thumb across my cheek and cupping his hand behind my head.

My heart began to race.

I touched my tongue to the tip of his, and we played hide and seek. He tangled his fingers into my hair and deepened the kiss.

I struggled to find air.

He backed me onto the couch, and we sank down. Touching, kissing. His warm breath on my neck made me shiver. A nice shiver.

Pulling the ribbons from my hair, he groaned softly in my ear.

I closed my eyes to enjoy a warm, dizzy feeling. A swirling around in the clouds feeling. A don't-ever-stop feeling.

Then he drew back.

"Please, Josh," I whispered, pulling him close again to nibble on the soft crest of his ear.

He kissed me once more. "I better take you home. Gina will be down in a sec."

I moaned to myself, then out loud.

Josh chuckled, and the stupid heat rose on my cheeks again.

He kissed me on the nose and held up the flute. "We'd better put this thing away. It's dangerous."

Dangerous? Not the flute?

Josh smiled at what must have been my confused expression.

"It's a courting flute, Forrest. A man plays this to win the heart of the woman he loves."

## CHAPTER 18

*The following Tuesday morning*

"Need any help?" I asked as I dumped my school pack and dodged around the bar.

"Nah," Rocky shoved the case of beer in the fridge and shot a thumb over his shoulder toward the back door. "Someone's waiting for you."

Starving after practice, I grabbed two bags of chips from the cash register and a couple of sodas.

Manny had his feet up on the old rocker in the garden. The cop accepted the soda with a smile, popped it and took a long draw. "You wanted to see me?"

I stood over the man, feet apart, shoulders squared. "When are you getting George out of jail?"

"He's doing fine, Josh. He's safe. I have someone on the inside making sure nothing happens to him."

"How many people are in on this investigation?"

"Several. But I can't say who. Or how many."

I crunched my chips for a moment. "Then this isn't just about Morty, is it?"

The cop twitched out a negative.

"How long's the investigation been going on?"

"Almost two years."

"No shit?"

"Not only here in Arizona." Manny sat up and leaned toward me. "This case is fairly recent. The team's working cases in other states too. Utah,

121

Colorado, even back east."

I grunted my surprise through a mouthful of chips. "So Morty's murder brought you into the investigation?"

Manny rubbed a hand over his rough-sounding beard. "In a way. Morty was the guy who got the team started on the case in Central Arizona. That's when I joined the group."

I pulled up a rusted lawn chair and sat.

"Morty'd been in on the plot awhile." Manny leaned back again. "Six months ago, he contacted someone, who knew someone, who knew someone in law enforcement. He said he wanted out. He was sick. Cancer. He wanted to make a deal. We offered him immunity, and money for treatment, if he helped us build a case against the rest of the smugglers."

I stopped chewing and let my chin drop, but my heart raced. "Wow. He was your informant?"

Manny blinked a quick yes with his eyes. "Was. But he hadn't told us much before he disappeared."

I almost choked. "So if Morty got killed…"

"Look, Josh." The man's sharp gaze narrowed, and he lowered his voice further. "These poachers aren't digging for a few illegal arrowheads to display on a bookcase. They're plundering sites and selling off the artifacts to foreign buyers for big money. People will pay thousands, even tens of thousands for an ancient pot. The price of an authentic, good-sized petroglyph…?" He held out his palms. "Astronomical."

I glanced down, forcing my cramped fists to relax. Picturing the Magician's saber-toothed cat chiseled off of its sacred place and hanging on someone's wall made my stomach lurch. "No reputable dealer…"

"These guys don't go through regular channels like your cousin George. Artifacts are sold on a black market, or smuggled out of the country."

"Why'd Morty really get murdered?"

"Not sure. These crooks are pretty sophisticated, but not usually violent. Guys like Morty find, and sometimes harvest, the items, but a middle man handles transport. Tough to say how many layers of protection there are between the creeps at the bottom and the creeps on the top of the heap. Those are the ones we're after," he said, pointing a finger at me for emphasis.

"And George somehow got in the way."

"The argument in front of the council scared the shit out of Morty. He freaked."

"Musta scared the head honcho, too."

Manny blew out an exasperated breath and rubbed a hand over his hair. "Morty was set to have a meeting with someone high up, but then he disappeared. We thought for a while he'd booked it. Taken off to live out his last days in peace."

I stood and paced between Rocky's carefully planted rows of lettuce and onions and hot peppers. "But instead he'd been murdered." I crumpled the empty chip bag and sorted through my options.

Would helping Manny cause more problems for George? My stomach shoved up into my chest, cutting off my air. And Forrest was involved, too. Maybe in danger. I couldn't protect them on my own. I needed help. Official help.

Manny dug in his shirt pocket for a dirty, folded piece of paper. He opened it and handed it to me. "Know this guy?"

I squinted at the grainy picture and recognized the

face. "That's Zalo."

"How do you know him?"

"Kinda a drifter. Young kid, an orphan. Hard to tell how old. He used to hang around the Trading Post off and on. George would give him work. Sweeping up. That kind of thing. He's almost two years younger than me, but he's been on his own for a while."

"Heard that."

"I don't think he went to school here in Verde. Might be from up north on the Hopi reservation. Is he in on the scheme?"

Manny folded the paper and stowed it. "Could be. Nobody's seen the kid in quite a while."

"Did he kill Morty?"

Manny stood and threw on his backpack. "Doubt it. Morty, no matter what everyone thought of him, was the only person who was good to Zalo. He kept the kid fed. Listened to his crazy stories."

I drained the last of my drink and crumpled the can underfoot. "Man. Do you think Zalo's dead, too?"

"Hope not."

The cop took a step in my direction. "You know something, Josh," he stated, but his voice was both stern and understanding. "You need to tell me everything."

I hesitated but then clicked my tongue. "I know where they're hiding the artifacts."

The man's left eyebrow rose at least an inch. "Where?"

I raised my chin. "Get George out first."

"Look, man…"

"No, that's the deal. When George is home and protected. Forrest and her Gran, too. Then I'll tell you."

Manny looped his hands on his belt and blew out a long breath. "I'll see what I can do.

## CHAPTER 19

George's hearing was scheduled for the following week. That day, I took the day off school, and Gina and Rocky closed up for the morning.

Forrest scooted in next to me on the slick courtroom bench. "Am I late?"

I shook my head and moved over to make more room. "George's prelim is next."

She leaned in and whispered in my ear. "He's getting out, right?"

"Hope so." I took her hand, and she squeezed my fingers.

The door behind the empty jury box opened, and a bored-looking officer led George across the courtroom.

I sucked in a harsh breath.

George rattled toward his seat wearing a bright orange jump suit, slippers, and chains. He smiled when he spotted me and raised a shackled hand in recognition.

I forced my face into a matching smile and waved in return.

Although I needed to puke, I closed my eyes and fisted my hands in my lap. How could they do this to George? How could Manny have let this happen?

Then the judge arrived, and Forrest pulled me to my feet when the bailiff shouted, "All rise."

Gina and Rocky hurried in as the judge called the

room to order.

The District Attorney, dressed in a I'm-a-tough-guy black suit, gleaming white shirt, and purple striped tie, stood and sauntered over to the witness box. He waited, rocking in his too-shiny shoes, while the bailiff swore in the first witness, Sheriff Robb.

"Lawyer's a tool," Forrest hissed in my ear.

I tried to listen, but I knew the frustrating story too well. It made me furious all over again to hear Robb recount the flimsy evidence. Yeah, yeah. George had no alibi. And he'd threatened Morty at the meeting. A few shafts of an eagle feather.

I searched the audience. Of course, Manny wasn't hanging around in the courtroom, but what do you bet the insider who worked with him was lurking somewhere in the crowd?

A chill prickled my shoulders and washed over my body like a flash flood. Was the murderer in the crowd, too? Watching?

I shifted in my seat. How could I know? How could I tell?

When Forrest took my hand in hers, her warmth fought back my shivers.

I moved closer to her. "Can you do it here?"

She gave me a puzzled scrunch of her eyes and mouth.

"You know. Hear the lies?"

Her head did the smallest of negative shakes.

"Try? Please?"

She chewed on the inside of her cheek like she wanted to say no, but then nodded.

I scooted over to give her room, while she perched her hands on the back of the empty bench in front of us.

No one would probably notice, but her face changed when she focused her energy. The color and texture of her skin was deeper, more vibrant.

My heart pounded so hard, I was sure she would hear it, but I didn't dare touch her, or even move, while she did her thing.

After a few moments, she dropped her hand and settled against my shoulder, her brow furrowed. "I can't. There are too many people, too much energy."

I glanced away for a minute to hide my disappointment.

"It's not like I have a laser beam and can zero in on someone," She narrowed her eyes as she glanced at Robb. "But someone's lying about something."

"The sheriff? No way."

She focused again, and concentration hardened her face. "Don't know. Could be him or that creepy DA. I can't sort out the truth from the maze of their thoughts."

I cupped her shoulder and gave it a squeeze. "We'll get a chance later."

"What about you?" Forrest hissed.

"Me?"

"Can you tell anything?"

"Not from here."

Forrest tapped her finger on her lip. "What if you touched it, I mean?"

"You mean take a read on the evidence?" I blew out a quick, frustrated breath. "Never happen. That stuff will be locked away as soon as the hearing is finished."

The DA sauntered over to his table and picked up a large, carefully labeled plastic bag. Inside was a gun. "Tell us, Sheriff Robb, when did you find this?"

The Sheriff examined the evidence. "About ten

days after we found the body. My deputy found the gun on the 29th of September."

"And is this the murder weapon?"

"Yes. The county forensic unit called the Colt a perfect match. The gun fired the shot that killed Morty Abrams. It's a rare gun, too. Old."

"Registered?"

"No."

"Where was the gun found, Sheriff?"

"In the town of…."

"We can't hear you, Sheriff."

Robb cleared his throat and moved closer to the microphone. "In Camp Verde, buried under a dumpster behind Main Street."

The DA walked over and stared down at George. Straightening the lapels of his jacket, the lawyer turned to face Robb. "And how close is the dumpster to the Trading Post owned by George Kwail?"

"Just down the block. But…"

The DA held up his hand to cut Robb off.

The sheriff bit his lip and glanced at George with pained frustration.

Cinching his bright purple tie, the lawyer drew practiced fingers through his blond hair. He turned toward the crowd. A smirk edged up one side of his thin mouth. "And were you able to identify the fingerprints on the gun?"

I twitched. Why did the creep sound so smug? That wasn't George's gun. He didn't even own a gun.

Robb glanced over at me, a reluctant expression shadowing his face for an instant. "Yes."

A buzz rippled through the spectators, and I shoved my knuckles into my mouth to keep from shouting. I practically leaped out of my seat, but Forrest squeezed my thigh.

"During discovery, I was told there were no prints," the DA continued. He placed the weapon back on his table.

Robb shifted and cleared his throat again. "At that point we had some smudged partials, but the FBI was finally able to match them. We received the results yesterday."

"And?" The DA drew out the word until it cut me like a razor.

"There's a sixty-eight percent chance the prints belong to the accused, George Kwail."

Someone in the crowd shouted.

I blinked my burning eyes. In the echo-y distance, the judge pounded his gavel, calling for order. I jumped up and dashed for the door. Would I make the men's room before I puked?

****

Pacing the old marble floor, Forrest greeted me in the hall outside the courtroom. The bathroom door squeaked, and I walked toward her, probably looking very green, my shoulders hunched, my gait unsteady. "Did the judge hold George over for trial?"

She gave me a quick nod, took my hand, and led me through the double doors into the fall sunshine. I shielded my eyes from the bright light and gave her a wan smile. It didn't take a mind reader to know I was in pain.

Gina hurried over and hugged me. Rocky stood behind her, his face cast in a fierce grimace.

"We need to find Zalo," I said, sounding steadier than I must have looked.

Rocky nodded. "Nobody has seen the kid since August."

"Exactly," I continued, suddenly feeling more resolute, more determined. "He's the witness we need."

Rocky rubbed his fuzzy chin. "Or the suspect."

"Zalo didn't do it," Forrest argued.

I turned to face her. "You knew him?"

"Kinda. We moved into the shop in August. Zalo was hanging around, and offered to load in some of the heavy stuff. Gran took a real liking to him. She was always feeding him. I didn't know anyone else, so sometimes we talked."

"He's wasn't too…you know… smart," I said.

She shot me a sharp glance. Ouch.

"You'd be surprised. He may not have had much school, but he knows all about the history of the valley. Knows all the native legends."

"Weird," I said.

"That's probably why Morty made friends with him," Forrest guessed aloud.

Rocky shrugged his beefy shoulders. "Morty may have used Zalo to find the artifacts."

"Do you think the poor boy's dead, too?" Gina asked.

Forrest looked as green as I'd felt a minute ago.

"Let's hope he's hiding somewhere." Rocky put his arm around his wife.

"If he's still alive," Forrest continued, sounding more hopeful, "and we can find him…."

She scuffed her shoes together. "Maybe he saw what happened."

"Or maybe he's the murderer."

## CHAPTER 20

*Three days later*

I paced Rocky's narrow garden, then turned to face the undercover cop. "Somehow, Zalo's in on this. Forrest said he knew all the old legends. We think Morty was using him to locate artifacts. You have to find him."

Manny checked his buzzing phone, thumbed in a brief message and said, "We've been trying. The chopper's been up since daybreak, searching the valley. Zip."

"Did you check the bus station? Maybe the cops in Flagstaff have seen him. Or Phoenix?"

Manny put up both hands in an irritating, listen-to-me-I'm-the-grown-up way. "Josh, sit. Listen to what I'm saying."

"I can't. Someone's framing George, and if I don't find out what's going on, he's going to be convicted. I need to prove he's innocent."

"That's my job."

I stopped pacing, crossed my arms and stuck out my chin. "Well, you're not doin' such a bang-up job."

Manny's face darkened with a deep frown. "Listen. Justice takes a very long time. It'll be months before George faces trial."

"And until then, he's sitting in a jail cell? That's crap."

"Then help me. Give me the information you have. How do you expect me to do my job when you're holding out on me?"

I stared at the frustrated man. What did it matter now? "The salt mine."

"Those old ones off Baker Road?"

"I saw some guys there one night."

"What were you doing out there at night?"

I ignored that question. No way would I tell Manny about the necklace or my ghost, but was I smart to hand over even this much info?

The cop sat silently, waiting.

"There are three mines. The smallest, the one farthest to the east, has a new iron door. Someone's keeping stuff there. Don't know what. I heard them loading, or maybe unloading a truck."

"When?"

"Right after George was arrested. Before I met you."

"How many guys?"

"Three, I think."

"You should have said something before," he grumbled. "I would've put eyes on the place."

"I've been watching. They haven't been back."

"Did they see you? Know you were there?"

"Nah, man." I shook my head.

"Might have been the guys from Flag picking up a load."

I froze, "You know about them?"

Manny rubbed his unshaven chin and nodded.

"Then why haven't you arrested them?"

"They didn't murder Morty. We've had a team watching them for months."

"I don't get it."

"They're low-level grunts. Little herrings." He flicked his finger in the air. "We can pick them up anytime. We're waiting, hoping to catch them when they make contact with someone higher up the food chain."

"You want the bigger fish?"

Manny nodded again. "More like the shark."

"And what's George? Chum?"

## CHAPTER 21

Room Six at the Connor was always so stuffy. I stuck the master key in my apron pocket, pushed back my bangs, and, holding my breath, marched across the room to throw open the old sash windows. I stared out over the park below for a moment, and drew in a breath of fresh air.

"Better," I said to myself. Before I gathered towels and clean linens from my cart, I checked out the damage the last slobs had done to the room and gave a long sigh.

I'd never finish. This room, the largest in the hotel, always looked like a tornado had blown through.

First I righted the lamp on the old mahogany dresser and stripped one of the beds. I straightened the pictures on the wall. Funny how every single one was tipped to the left. I rubbed a chill off my arms. "Damn place must be haunted."

I glanced at the old-fashioned clock by the bed. Better hurry. Josh was waiting for me at Rocky's.

Because I always left the door to any room partway open, I heard the man's voice as soon as he stepped into the hall.

"No," he shouted clearly as he stomped down the corridor my way.

The guy sounded afraid, so I edged closer to the door and pretended to polish the ornate mirror on the wall.

His footsteps passed the room, but the next words he spoke into his phone were garbled.

I peeked into the hall and gathered soaps and lotions I didn't need. It was the man who'd checked in last night.

Short, thin, way past thirty, he was wearing a suit, like he worked in a city. Mr. Smith. I let out a little snort. Right. Super-creative name.

Did I have time to catch a reading from him before he got to the stairs at the end of the hall?

Ducking behind my cart, I closed her eyes, put out a hand, and gave it a shot.

*Anger. Lots of anger, but under the fury there was a layer of cold fear.*

Definitely hiding something. Something big. This guy was scared. I focused my mind.

"What're you doing?"

When I glanced up, my heart went into overdrive, racing like Tilley did on the road to Jerome. Mr. Smith loomed over me, his mean, dark eyes squinting, and his pockmarked face twisted with suspicion.

I rose part way and tucked a strand of hair behind my ear. "Nothing, sir."

"Are you spying on me?"

I stood and brushed my apron with one damp hand. "What for, sir? My pen rolled under my cart." I twirled my ponytail and dropped a stupid expression onto my face, staring at him with a blank gaze.

Smith glared at me another second, then turned and stomped away.

I didn't breathe until the exit door slammed at the bottom of the stairs. Then I dashed for the window and put out both hands.

Could I read someone from this far away? I grimaced and pushed my focus to the limit. Yes. There was the fear. I reached out, gathering any thoughts.

A rough sketch of a saber-toothed cat formed in my mind, and my stomach did a flip. Cat? Like the one on Josh's necklace? I swallowed hard.

Smith moved out of range and beeped entry to his blue Honda.

I leaned against the sill, breathing hard.

I ran down the stairs and into the bar. I needed to tell Josh.

\*\*\*\*

"Are you sure it was the same cat?" I yelled over the wind while I buckled my seat belt and grabbed the chicken bar.

Forrest shifted into third and revved the engine. "Come on, come on," she shouted at Tilley. The jeep sputtered, then shot forward, racing through the narrow streets of town.

Ignoring the speed limit and a small gaggle of angry tourists who had to dodge out of the way, we roared through town. Soon we were climbing the steep mountain road on the west side of Jerome.

The blue Honda, with Smith at the wheel, was several switchbacks ahead.

The road above town wound through heavy scrub forest, at times blocking the view of our quarry. She pushed Tilley faster.

"Don't get too close." I stood and braced myself on the windshield support. The wind blew back my hair.

"I know, I know." She gripped the wheel.

"Forrest? What about the cat?"

"It was the same cat," she said, keeping her eyes forward. "Not silver and turquoise like your necklace. More like a drawing, black and red. Like it'd been scratched into…"

"Rock?" I plopped in my seat and closed my eyes. "They're after the petroglyph."

She glanced at him, then returned her focus to the road. "You know it?"

I grimaced. "Yeah. It belongs to the Magician."

She swallowed hard. "Sacred?"

"Very." I nodded, feeling green again.

"Right. We'll follow this shmuck and find out what's going on. Then we can turn him and his compadres in to the sheriff."

Forrest pushed the pedal to the floor mat. Tilley kicked out gravel and leaned heavily into the next ninety-degree turn.

I spotted the car on the hairpin curve above us. The blue Honda was more than a mile ahead, but we wouldn't lose him. There were no turnoffs along here.

She stomped the clutch to downshift for the next climb, but Tilley didn't respond. The gears ground, and a strange screeching noise came from underneath the jeep. Blue-grey smoke billowed out the back.

"No-o," Forrest cried, punching the gas again. Nothing. We sputtered to the next turnout, barely. Tilley gasped and coughed and died.

I stared up the hill. The Honda rounded the last curve and roared out of sight.

Hands clutching the wheel, Forrest sat in the quiet for a moment before the first tear trickled down her cheek. She brushed it away. "I'm s-sorry, Josh."

I reached over and took her hand. "Nothing we can

do now." With a deep sigh, I climbed out my side. My feet crunched on the gravel as I rounded the jeep and opened her door. "Let's roll her farther into the turnout so she's safe. Then we'll hike back to town. Rocky can help us get her running again."

"But we lost Smith."

I raked my fingers through my hair in frustration, but gave her a half smile. "I'll go talk to the sheriff first thing in the morning. At least we know the guy's name. And what he's after."

## CHAPTER 22

I skipped practice after school and hitched a ride over to the police station. When I rapped on the sheriff's door, Robb gave an offhanded wave through his office window, and I peeked in.

"Hey there, Josh." The sheriff grinned and flipped his poker chip once, and then twice, in the air. "Come down to see George?"

"Yeah. At least the judge let him stay here." I entered the sheriff's cluttered office and moved the only available chair, an old oak job that must have weighed a ton and took up the corner of the room. I shoved the chair over in front of the sheriff's beat-up desk. "I needed to talk to you first."

"Sure. Sure." Robb frowned for an instant. The chip flipped again. "What's up?"

I settled into the chair, but my hands fidgeted in my lap. Cold sweat trickled down the back of my already clammy T-shirt. Feeling hyped, I stood up and paced the room. Although I'd wrestled all the way over with what to tell Robb, I still hadn't reached a decision that felt right.

Chewing on my lip, I made another lap of the small room. Why had Manny insisted Forrest and I keep quiet about the ring of thieves? Or what his team was investigating? Sure, it was a Federal case, and Robb wasn't part of it, but....

I frowned and wedged my hands in my pockets, still pacing.

Robb continued to flip the red chip, his cool eyes watching me intently.

I rubbed the back of my neck. I needed to do something. And even though I'd stayed up most of the night waiting and watching, Smith never returned to the hotel. Worse, Manny was nowhere to be found. He hadn't answered his phone or called me back since Tuesday.

I tugged on the bottom of my shirt and turned to the sheriff. "Do you have any new leads?"

Robb shook his head.

"Has Zalo turned up?"

The sheriff rose and tucked one hand into his duty belt. "Sit down, Josh. I can see you're upset. Why don't you let me get you something to drink? Okay? That'll give you a sec to calm down and tell me what's on your mind."

I nodded. The breath I drew hitched on the way in, and then on the way out, but I stopped pacing. "Yeah." I needed to calm down. George needed me to help, not flip out.

The sheriff tossed his poker chip on the desk and left the office. His footsteps echoed down the hall. The door to the break room opened and closed.

Pacing his office again, I stopped behind the battered desk. I picked up Robb's lucky chip and flipped it a few times. Anything to help myself concentrate.

When the chip landed, it burned my palm, and I hissed in a breath.

*Dark, flowing knowledge.*

A vision flooded into my head that my shields couldn't block. I almost fell over, and had to grab Robb's chair to stay on my feet. I pushed back the darkness, but the vision leaked into my consciousness. The desperation surrounded me. Swallowed me.

I threw down the disc and rubbed my palm.

When I was under control again, I stared at the red chip. I needed to know. Ignoring the fear choking me, I let down my shields and reached out my hand.

*Smoke clouded a dimly lit room, and I tasted the bitterness of liquor on my tongue. A green felt table, cards.*

*Disappointment.*

*Fear.*

I drew in a long, quaking breath. Robb was a gambler? So? Everyone had secrets. Vices. I should stop. This wasn't my business.

My hand trembled, but I closed my eyes again.

*"How could three kings not win the hand?" Robb shouted. His voice sounded like he might cry. "I've been cheated."*

*Other men laughed and gathered the money and chips scattered over the table. Lots of money.*

*Thick grey fog blurred the scene, but then cleared to bright sunlight and dazzling heat.*

*Robb stood on a high cliff. It had rained the night before. I recognized the sharp scent of the creosote bushes.*

*Another man stood close by, but I couldn't*

*see his face. They shouted.*

*Frustration.*

*Anger.*

*Then terror.*

*Cold, hungry, overpowering terror.*

I threw down the chip and bolted for the door. After fumbling with the door handle, I dashed into the hall, almost running into Robb.

"Hey. Where ya going?" The Sheriff chuckled, holding up the cans of soda.

"Forgot something." I called over my shoulder, trying to keep my voice calm.

"Catch ya later, then."

I turned at the exit door and stared at the man. I could have sworn it was fear etching furrows across Robb's face.

\*\*\*\*

"It's too dangerous," Forrest yelled, following me through the school parking lot. She grabbed me by the arm and tried to pull me out of the driver's side of her jeep. "What a mule-headed idiot. You don't even know how to drive."

"Do too." I pushed her hand away. "I learned last summer in California, but I'm not old enough to take the test."

"Then let me go with you."

I shook my head and ground the starter. "We don't know who to trust. Robb's in on it somehow. Who knows, maybe Manny is, too."

Forrest stepped back. "Josh, you're scaring me."

A cold chill shook my shoulders and crawled down my spine. I'd frightened her. Well, I was scared, too.

Damn. I was petrified.

"I won't let you go and get yourself killed." Calmly, she walked to the back of her jeep and stood between me and the driveway, so I was stuck in the parking place, and couldn't pull forward without smashing another car.

"Move, Forrest," I yelled as I watched her in the rearview mirror.

She planted her feet right next to the bumper and shook her head. "Talk to me, Josh. Tell me what's going on. Then I'll give you Tilley. Or I'll take you anywhere you ask."

I glared at her once more in the mirror, but then dropped my chin onto my chest.

Before I had a chance to reconsider, she dashed around, grabbed the keys from the ignition and let out a breath. "You're such a dope."

I crossed my arms and grimaced at the steering wheel. Tears blurred my vision. "My mom used to say that. Mostly she was teasing, but sometimes I understood she was afraid for me."

Forrest reached down and kissed me gently on the cheek. Her warm skin smelled of sunshine.

With a long groan, I pushed out of the seat, stood, and wrapped my arms around her.

"You scared me." She put her head down on my chest. Her heart was beating even faster than mine.

"Come on. Let's find a quiet place to talk," she said

I kissed her gently on her forehead, before releasing her. "You're right. We need a plan."

# CHAPTER 23

*The following week*

I chewed on my pinky nail and stared out my bedroom window into the black night. Had I done the right thing, going along with Josh's totally insane plan? My heart constricted until the pain brought stinging tears to my throat and eyes. What if our idea didn't work? What if the big lug got hurt?

I threw myself on my bed, crossed my arms, and let out a long, frustrated sigh. It took days longer to pull our plan together than we'd figured.

Days of sneaking around. Days of lying to everyone. Days of worrying about Josh. But I only needed to wait one more night. Ten and one-half more freaking hours.

Josh left Jerome after dark to recover the treasure from its hiding place in the salt mine. I would have tagged along, even gone back into his horrible, haunted cave, but that meant even more lies. Gran was suspicious enough already. We'd decided I would stay home and try to act "normal" for a change.

I stared up at the ceiling and watched the fan circle endlessly. Even with it whirling at full speed, the room felt stifling. Had I done the right thing? Wished Mom was here. It was times like these I missed my mom the most.

I closed my eyes and brought forward the only

clear memory I had of my mother.

*I tasted the salt of the ocean. Felt the grit of the warm sand under my small, chubby legs.*

I smiled. I couldn't have been more than three, playing with a yellow plastic bucket and an old spoon.

*Mama laughed and patted the sand into a tower. "I'm building a castle for my princess," she said. My mother's face was young, her skin smooth, burnished from the sun and the salty air. The sea breeze whipped her long ponytail.*

*Then a man spoke behind her. I couldn't see him in the late afternoon light, and only remembered a pair of shiny black shoes. Suddenly my mother wasn't smiling anymore.*

*The man took Mama by the arm. I put up my hands. I felt scared and wanted a hug. A hug from my mother.*

*Then Mama started crying and walked away with the man, and I cried, too.*

"Witness protection." Gran explained when I was old enough to understand the words.

I swallowed the lump in my throat and squeezed my eyes shut.

"Someday, sweetheart," Gran had whispered. "Someday, your mama can come home. Until then, we have each other."

I rolled over and stared at the scarred floorboards of my tiny room. I couldn't tell anyone. Not even Josh. If anyone knew about my mother, she and Gran could be found. They'd be killed. The secret kept my mother and grandmother safe. I rubbed my stinging eyes.

It was a hard secret to keep, *especially* from Josh, and his gift made him even more dangerous. I'd already hidden everything belonging to my mother, just in case he touched it and saw the truth.

****

At exactly three o'clock the next afternoon, I stood on the side of a low-ceilinged room in the local museum. In front of me, a crowd huddled around a glass display case. I glanced around. Would Smith return to see the treasure?

Through the open doors, more media shoved into the main exhibit area of the tiny historical museum. Up at the podium, Josh stood next to the curator and squinted into video camera lights.

A woman reporter in a too-short-for-those-legs red business suit shouted a question above the jostle. "Where'd you find the necklace?"

Josh leaned forward to speak into the gaggle of microphones on the lectern. "In a hidden cave." His voice sounded calm, but worry lines framed his mouth. He scanned over the heads of the crowd. Was Josh looking for Smith? Or Robb?

"Anything else in that cave?" another reporter's raspy voice yelled from the other side of the room.

"Maybe."

The pushy woman in red reasserted her rights to the interview. "Who owns the treasure?"

"Our tribe." Josh turned to the locked case displaying his ancient silver and turquoise necklace. The large pendant mosaic glowed softly in the light. "This is an ancient relic of the Cat Clan."

"How old?"

He gave a theatrical shrug. "Almost a thousand years."

Someone in the middle of crowd whistled above the appreciative murmur.

The museum curator joined Josh at the podium.. I glanced at the floor to hide my smile.

Behind thick glasses, the woman's gleaming eyes and tiny, tense body telegraphed her excitement.

The curator cleared her throat three times and tapped on the microphone before speaking. "Thank you for attending this news conference. Mr. Kwail has made an important discovery. We will be authenticating the find with the university. Our local expert has already examined the artifact and has preliminarily stated the piece was made about 1100 AD."

Another long murmur filtered through the room, and I moved closer to the side door. I still didn't recognize anyone in the crowd.

"What's it worth?" a man in the front shouted.

I stood on tiptoe and searched the room. Was that Smith? Casually, I sidled toward the voice.

"Priceless," the curator replied, a pleased smile on her thin lips.

Heading to the opposite side of the room, I dodged between a pack of reporters madly texting into their uber-phones, but a large hand grabbed my arm. I would have yelled, but Manny gave me the don't-make-a-peep-sign with a finger to his lips and pulled me outside. Once through the door, he hauled me over to the corner of the wooden porch fronting the building.

Brow furrowed, mouth grim, he looked mad. No, super-pissed. He loomed his mega-sized body over me like he could intimidate me.

Fat chance.

I didn't flinch, but darted out from his grasp. Time to go on the offensive. "Where the hell—heck—have you been?" I kept the volume of my voice under control, but hissed with anger.

Manny blinked, and then moved closer to get in my face. "Working." He matched his angry tone to mine. "Trying to solve this freaking case. Trying to keep you and your idiot boyfriend alive."

Two more reporters stomped up the steps into the museum. Manny fumed until they were inside.

"We've been calling you for days." I got right up in his space and lowered my voice even more "We found someone in the ring. Maybe a buyer. He was at the hotel."

Manny's brow furrows deepened.

"Yeah. Smith. Medium height and build. Ugly face. Prissy suits. We've been tailing him for months."

My jaw dropped, but I quickly yanked it back into position.

"Although you two idiots blew it the other day when you followed him out of Jerome. He'd spotted you, so my guys had to drop back. It took us until this morning to track him down again."

"You caught him?"

"Sorta. He's dead."

The sky tipped. Good thing an old rocking chair sat next to me on the porch. I grabbed the arm and slumped into the seat.

"Did we…" I sucked in air, but the nausea rose higher in my throat.

"No. You didn't have anything to do with his murder."

A cool wind blew across my damp skin, and I swallowed the sour taste in my mouth.

Manny paced for a moment while I breathed deeply and regained my balance. He leaned against the porch railing and crossed his ankles. The anger leaked out of his face and his stance. He almost seemed relaxed. Almost. But his eyes never stopped searching the crowd through the window behind me.

I grimaced and took the chance of doing a quick read. Interesting.

"Smith was an idiot," he continued. "Low-level grunt. Someone who bought and sold the artifacts. Took his cut. Not the head honcho."

"Whoever's running this operation is silencing the people involved," Josh said from a few feet away.

I jumped at the sound of his voice. I hadn't heard him approach, but he must have listened to the end of our conversation.

Manny tipped his chin higher. "You've scared him. Scared him shitless."

Finally I refocused my vision, mostly because Josh was holding my hand. "What should we do?"

"We follow our plan." Josh turned to face the cop. "We're using the necklace for bait, and we'll catch the bastard when he comes to steal it."

Manny spit over the railing. "Really stupid, kid."

"Then you do better," Josh shouted.

I pulled Josh toward me. "Calm down, Josh. We need Manny's help."

"He could be part…"

"No, we can trust him," I said evenly. I touched my hand to his chest and signaled him with a small burst of my energy.

Josh took a moment to reconsider, then swallowed and nodded. He lowered his voice to a real whisper and faced the lawman again. "We know who's behind this."

"Who?"

"Not yet."

The lawman sputtered with frustration.

"Soon," I offered.

"Not a guess. I'll need real proof." Manny said.

Josh assumed his macho stance. "We'll give you all the proof you need."

I pressed my hands against my thighs. Too late to play coy. "We broke into the museum two nights ago and installed extra video cameras. Even upgraded the retro one on the door. We can watch every angle in the museum from Josh's room."

"Borrowed them from George…sort of." Josh confessed. "He bought the cameras months ago for the trading post, but I hadn't gotten around to installing them."

Manny groaned and ground his jaw back and forth. He pounded his fist on the railing a few times before he turned and faced us. "And this mastermind isn't going to figure out your frigging trap? You'll get yourselves killed."

My pulse still raced in my brain, fuzzing the edges of what I could read, but his expression had changed to the feral look of a wolf. "Josh," I said. "Let's try this his way."

"Are you crazy? Forrest…he has nothing."

"Listen." Manny said, but it sounded more like a growl.

"No, you listen," Josh argued. "If you want in, it's our plan. Our deal."

"I'll haul you in on obstruction charges."

"Go ahead, try." Josh glanced at the door to the museum. "I have quite a following right now."

Looking disgusted, the cop waved his hand in the air. "Then I'll leave you to it. Maybe your buddy, the sheriff, will help you out when you catch the killer in your stupid trap."

I shook his arm. "Josh. Please. I'm scared."

"He's playing us."

I squinted at Manny for a long moment. "Noooo. He's not."

"Damn it, Forrest. Are you sure? After all the planning, all the work we did to get this far?"

"I'm sure." I said with absolute confidence. "We should let Manny do his job."

I smiled a brief smile. Had Josh caught my signal?

# CHAPTER 24

"Boy, you are so thick sometimes, Colonel Mustard." I rubbed my hands on my thighs and gulped in some air to calm my pulse.

"Thick?" Josh rose along with his voice. "I don't get it. What were you thinking? Why would we let Manny take over now?" he demanded when the cop was out of earshot. Sitting on the railing, Josh kicked the spindles with an angry, rhythmic thump. "We had a plan."

I giggled and reached up to give him a peck on the cheek. "And it worked."

He narrowed his eyes. "You trust him, right?"

"Oh, yeah. Manny's one of the good guys. That I know, but he's hiding something. Something really big."

He took me gently by the shoulders and leaned down to meet my gaze. "Are we still going through with the trap?"

"We have to. No one else can do this, Josh. It's up to us." I recognized the excitement in my voice.

"It's a risk."

"We have no choice."

"Did you see Robb today?"

I gulped. "No, but he might have been somewhere in the crush."

Josh stood silent for a long moment, then nodded.

"Could you read anyone else?"

I shook my head. "Tough with a ton of reporters in the room." I pulled my hair into a knot and waited for him to continue. When he didn't, I chuckled. "Amazing how fast you can spread the word about a treasure these days."

He gave me a quick nod, but his mind was somewhere beyond the porch.

I nudged his arm. "What about your ghost?"

Josh focused on my face. "He knows, and he's okay with the plan."

I released a sigh. "Good. Last thing we need is an angry spook."

He led me toward the front stairs.

"Will he protect his necklace?" I asked in a low hiss.

"Without a doubt. My ghost and those new security cameras."

I gave a nervous giggle and more of the tension seeped out of me. "I'm starved. Let's go get Gran and hit the Haunted Hamburger for something to eat. Nothing's going to happen in the middle of the day."

"You think the paparazzi will leave us alone?" Josh made a short, disgusted sound and pointed to the reporters still milling around the street in front of the Jerome Historical Museum. "Forget it."

I dropped my shoulders and made a face. "Then I guess we're stuck with kale soup."

One of the reporters must have seen us. He gave a shout and two photographers headed in our direction.

Josh grabbed my hand, and we dodged around the side of the museum, jumped the porch railing, and hurried down the steep alley. We waited for traffic to clear, and then dashed across the street and into Gran's tiny shop.

Josh pulled me into the sweet-smelling downstairs room, closed the door with care and wrapped his arms around my waist. "No one here," he whispered lightly into the curve of my ear.

His smile forged bolts of heat around my heart.

I closed my eyes, and met his lips with mine. Soft. Wonderful lips. He pulled me to him, and power seared through every nerve and muscle in my body. My tongue tasted his, and the strange and wonderful sensations grew and heated.

I took a couple of quick gasps of air, and then, wrapping my arms around his neck, moved in for another, longer, more intense kiss.

We were both panting by the time I pulled back. Gently, I touched his cheek with my fingertips. His eyes were almost black, a pale rim of amber edging his wide-open irises.

I tunneled my fingers through his thick hair, not needing to read his thoughts to know exactly what was going on in his all-male, teenage brain. Pretty much the same thoughts were swirling around in mine.

His palms slipped down my spine with strokes that echoed my own need.

"For-rest? Is that you, baby?"

With a groan, Josh dropped his hands.

When he let go of me, it was like falling to earth from the clouds. I landed hard and needed a moment to pull myself together.

A footstep sounded on the top wooden stair. "Forrest? Is Josh with you? Can you come up here for a minute?"

Josh shot me a smile, and my heart leaped back into overdrive. I almost grabbed him again. Who cared if Gran walked into the room?

With a knowing grin, Josh tipped his head toward the stairs.

I sighed. "Sure, Gran. Can Josh stay for dinner?"

He squeezed my hand, and we hurried up. I didn't glance up until we'd reached the landing, and I saw two pairs of shoes.

\*\*\*\*

The sheriff held a gun on Angel Wings.

I sucked in half a breath before my throat closed. Forrest stood next to me, very still. Very pale. Her hand went cold in mine and started to tremble.

"Gran?" she whispered.

"He made me. He said he'd kill you if I didn't call you up here," Angel Wings sobbed. A tear dripped off her chin.

"Move," Robb ordered, his voice cold and very calm. He pointed his service revolver toward the kitchen table in the middle of the room.

With a quick jerk, the sheriff backed up his hostage and allowed us to pass.

I guided Forrest ahead of me, shielding her from Robb. We reached the table.

"Now sit," he ordered.

She hadn't let go of my hand, and the shaking increased. I was having trouble not shaking myself. We pulled out chairs and sat, facing the man and his pitiful hostage.

Angel Wing's whole body shook, and her face went gray when Robb jammed the gun against her temple.

The sheriff glanced around the room, his eyes restless. No fear showed on his face, or in his manner. His hand and the gun were steady. He pushed Angel Wings toward the table. "There." He pointed to the empty chair next to Forrest.

With a quiet sob, Angel Wings ran to join us. "I'm so sorry, baby."

Forrest grabbed the terrified woman's hands. "Shh, it's okay, Gran. You couldn't have done anything else, really."

Without lowering his weapon, Robb leaned against the kitchen wall. "And I thought you were clever, Josh. What an idiotic move. Displaying the necklace. Trying to bait me. Stupid. Did she talk you into it?" He waved the gun in Forrest's direction.

I made my best derisive noise, leaning back in the chair and resting one ankle on my knee. "All my idea. These two? Right. They're not clever enough to plot their way out of a Wal-Mart bag."

Forrest gave me a filthy look. One that would have sliced me clean through if I didn't know it was playacting.

"Let them go." I held up my palms, then crossed my arms slowly. "It's me you want. Not them. I'm the one who can help you."

Forrest let out a long, plaintive cry, and then brushed a fake tear from her eye. She dropped her head into her hands. "Please, Josh. Don't show him the real treasure. Please. You can't."

Angel Wings moaned softly and curled an arm gently around her granddaughter's shoulder.

Robb shook his head. Keeping the gun pointed in our direction, he turned to the woman. "You got duct tape?"

Angel Wings sniffed out a nod.

"Get it."

Her purple caftan rippling with her trembles, Angel Wings moved toward the desk and pulled out a roll of bright orange tape.

Robb snorted. "Figures."

He tossed the roll toward me. "Tape the old lady to the chair. Tight. Hands and feet."

I rose and followed orders.

"I'll check it, so do it right."

Angel Wings cooperated, and I finished the job. I ripped off another section. "I'll do Forrest, too."

"No. You're both coming with me."

"I told you, she knows nothing."

Robb smiled. A big, important, I-got-this-all-figured-out smile. "Yeah, but you love her. And that, my young friend, will come in very handy."

****

Josh sat next to me in the sheriff's SUV. Silent.

The handcuffs bit into my wrist. I shifted my weight to my left side to ease the pain shooting up my arm.

I didn't need to use my gift to know what he was thinking about. Anger etched every line in his forehead and disappointment carved his mouth into a tense frown.

I nudged him with my leg. "Josh," I whispered. "What do we do now?"

"Don't worry," he said.

"Gran?"

"She'll be okay."

I nodded and dropped my chin. The night was

black. No moon. Clouds obscured even the weak light of the stars. Footsteps tromped across in the gravel, and I tensed again. My heart rate thudded in my brain. Robb.

The sheriff slammed shut the driver's side door and turned to face us. Shadows from the metal grill bolted between us hid his face. "Be light in an hour."

"You'll never get away with this," I said. My voice sounded steady, but my whole body trembled.

"Trite, little girl. Very trite. I've been getting away with 'this' for years." Robb pushed a button on the dash and the engine roared. "I've got four-wheel on this monster. Nothing can stop us now." He rubbed his hands together like some fiend in a horror movie. "Lead me to the treasure."

Josh glared at the man but didn't answer.

When Robb pointed the big revolver at Josh's face, my pulse went bananas, and cold sweat beaded on my neck. "Tell him."

"Let her go. Then I will," Josh said through clenched teeth.

"Again, my friend, you are not in a position to negotiate." Robb moved the gun slowly until I could see down the huge black hole of the barrel.

My breath stopped and the sweat pouring between my shoulder blades iced into crystals. I bit down on my lip to keep from crying out, and the taste of blood filled my mouth.

****

"Wait," I shouted, and moved in front of Forrest to block Robb's shot. "Take the road down to the valley. Get on the main highway. Head north of the casino." I made sure my voice sounded defeated.

"Good choice."

Robb drove with patience and skill. He said nothing until the lights of the casino flashed in the distance.

"Now what?" the Sheriff demanded.

I glanced at Forrest. She'd been quiet since we started the drive, and the trembling I'd felt through my leg had almost stopped. "It's okay," I thought to her. "We'll follow the plan." Would she catch the message?

She nudged me lightly and flashed me a one-sided smile. Even handcuffed, I wanted to reach over and kiss her. I let out a long, quiet sigh. That one kiss would probably end up getting us both killed.

I gave her a slow, meaningful nod, and then said to the sheriff, "Turn off at this next exit. Take Murphy road. It's still several miles out. Past the sacred mountain."

"Sacred mountain," Robb snickered. "What a load of bull."

A thin rim of golden light glowed on the eastern hills and lit the clouds along the horizon to magenta and purple. We drove through the open dessert. Huge, many-armed saguaros stood guard on the hilltops.

The road became rougher. Out past the river trail, it turned to gravel. We bounced over potholes and rattled over the washboard road until the path deteriorated and became almost too narrow for the big truck to pass.

Robb swore as he rolled the SUV over another large boulder.

"Left up here," I said.

"On top of the mesa?"

"Yeah."

Robb geared down, and the truck climbed steeply

toward the top of the pass. "You better not be lying."

I fought to balance myself so I didn't fall against Forrest every time we hit another washout. My body ached with exhaustion. With fear.

Was I a fool? Had I risked too much—not only my own life, but Forrest's, too? What if I failed, and Robb pillaged the Magician's treasure? Would my people suffer yet again?

And what about George? George would be left to rot in jail for crimes he hadn't committed. Gina and Rocky would wait for us to return and never know what happened. Angel Wings, too. How would she survive without Forrest's calm strength?

I struggled against the handcuffs until warm blood trickled down my thumb.

We reached the top of the mesa. Freaking little choice now. I had to trust the Magician would have my back. "Ok. See that cattle skull? There. To the right?"

Robb grunted.

"Park there. We walk the rest of the way."

The boughs of a piñon pine scraped the side of the truck. Robb stomped the emergency brake and got out. He opened my door and waved his gun.

"Forrest doesn't know where we're going. Lock her in. Let her stay in the truck while I show you."

"Not a chance, kiddo."

I ground my teeth at the man's sarcastic tone, but climbed out. Forrest scooted over and jumped down beside me.

"We have to go down the cliff edge," I warned. "It's a thousand-foot drop. We can't climb down without using our hands."

Robb studied me for a long moment. Frowning, he

shifted his weight from one foot to the other and rubbed one hand over the stubble on his jaw. Eyeing me with a hateful gaze, he unlocked Forrest's cuffs.

Handing her the key, Robb shoved her forward. "Free him."

Her hands shook, but she managed to undo my cuffs.

I wiped the blood off my sore wrists.

"You lead." Robb waved the gun toward the cliff. "And remember, I have your little friend. Any trick…" He wrapped his hand into Forrest's bright hair. "Do anything stupid, and I'll push her over the edge."

Forrest struggled against Robb's grip. "You'd never get away with murder. Someone would come hunting for us. My grandmother…"

When he yanked her hair, Forrest cried out.

"Think I care about taking out one more hippy-dippy shyster who sets up a woo-woo shop and cheats people? Don't cooperate, and I'll kill the old lady, just like I'll kill you. Now shut up and get moving."

"Someone would find us." Her voice quivered.

"Hah! Like who? All I need to do is leave your phones somewhere with a conversation of tender texts. "Please, Josh. I need you." He imitated Forrest's high voice. "Run away with me."

Robb chuckled, seeming pleased with his cleverness. "They'll never find us. I love you," he continued in an overdramatic, masculine tone.

Burning with fury, I fisted my hands and stepped closer.

Robb reacted. "I promise," he hissed, pointing the gun at Forrest. "I. Will. Kill. Her."

Palms toward him, hands splayed, I backed away.

"You'll never be sheriff after this."

"Like I care?" His laugh bounced off the dark red cliffs across the canyon. "After I grab this treasure, I'll have so much money, I can disappear. Who needs that job, anyway?"

I stared at my dusty feet and smiled. "We'll need a rope."

## CHAPTER 25

I slid down the steep trail to the first ledge. Forrest was behind me, and then Robb. When I clutched the overhanging bough of an old, twisted pine, the rough bark gouged my palms. I was sweating like I'd done a couple hundred crunches.

The morning breeze blew up the front of the mesa, and a sudden chill overtook me. Above the canyon, two golden eagles soared on updrafts, hunting.

A slow, pulsing drumbeat pounded in my brain, but it wasn't my heart. I found my footing and glanced over my shoulder.

Robb still had the gun pointed at Forrest. She half skidded, half shuffled down to the first ledge and stopped next to me.

She looked up. "Wow," she whispered.

A hundred feet above us, the red and black walls of the sheer rock cliff had been decorated with a thousand petroglyphs. Drawings of an ancient tribe who hunted the deer and elk of the canyon. Symbolic birds and snakes and people moved across the space.

"Keep going," Robb grunted.

Dodging the piles of wicked cholla and bright red prickly pear fruit, I helped Forrest over the gap between two rocks.

"Now move back."

We complied, standing in a tiny grotto under the

cliff face. Water dripped from a spring hidden in the rocks.

Robb negotiated the jump and edged to within a few feet of us. He was breathing hard, but his hand was steady on the gun. "Where to now?"

"Down," I said. "There's a ledge below us."

Robb tossed me the rope.

****

"Sit on that rock," Robb shouted at me from the ledge thirty feet above. "There. The one hanging over the cliff. And keep your hands on your head."

I did as I was told. My palms stung with rope burns, and my heart was pounding even louder than the deep drumbeat echoing in my brain. Furtively, I glanced up at the solar calendar, the huge, round, spiral petroglyph etched into the dark red wall of the lower ledge. Shivers sprinted up and down my spine.

I swallowed away the putrid taste in my mouth. What if the Magician wouldn't open the cave? Today wasn't the solstice. The sacred day when I entered the cave before wasn't for almost a month. And anyway, I didn't have the necklace.

What an idiot I was. The artifacts in the burial cave would be safe, but what would Robb do to us when he couldn't pillage the treasure?

Gun waving in the air, Robb pushed Forrest forward, and she started her overhand climb down the rope.

"Take it slow," I called, and she nodded. "Use that branch to brace yourself."

She rappelled down the first twenty feet, and was doing fine, but she slipped the last few and landed in a dusty heap.

I jumped up to help her, and a bullet danced off the rock in front of me. With a shout, I dodged back.

"Told you to sit," Robb said in a cool tone.

Scrambling to her feet, Forrest brushed the dirt from her jeans. "I'm fine."

I held up my hands and returned to my seat. Even from here, I could see the sheen of sweat on Robb's upper lip. The man was breathing hard.

"Sit on his lap," Robb shouted at Forrest.

I held her tightly. This might be the last time, ever. We breathed in sync and clung to each other.

Robb took the rope in one hand and held the gun in the other. "If either of you move, I'll shoot you both."

"He's got the necklace," Forrest whispered in my ear. "He must have stolen it when he left us in the car."

I nodded and squeezed her hand, but my gut dropped.

Robb landed on the ledge, and his heavy boots crunched in the gravel. He glanced around. "I don't see any cave."

"It's closed."

"Then open it."

"Can't. It's not the right time and I don't have…"

"What? This?" Robb pulled the necklace of the saber-toothed cat from inside his shirt.

I swallowed hard. "How'd you know?"

"Zalo." Robb chuckled and waved the necklace in the air. "Good ol' Zalo was full of stories. And Morty wasn't the only one he told. Such crap, but I listened to all those stupid legends. There was this one about a powerful Magician who owned a magic necklace and…."

"Where's Zalo?" Forrest interrupted.

"Yeah, well." Robb glanced out at the circling eagles and gave a long, dramatic-sounding sigh.

"Did you hurt him?"

Even in the growing heat of the morning, the cold message in the Sheriff's eyes gave me a shiver.

"Let's say I sent him off through the desert with enough water to survive, but I doubt he did."

I licked my lips, but my mouth went dry and sour. "Poisoned water? Right?"

Forrest whipped around. "From the well? You killed that poor kid with poisoned water from Montezuma's Well?" She glared at the Sheriff. I grabbed her to keep us both from getting shot. She quivered in my arms.

"Zalo was helpless." I shook my head.

"He knew too much," Robb shouted. "He saw…"

"He saw what happened to Morty," I finished the sentence. "You killed him?"

"It was an accident. He grabbed my gun. What could I do?"

"Why?" Forrest asked. "You have a son. A good job."

"He was in crazy debt," I explained. "Owed that shark at the casino, didn't you? That's how your addiction started. Years ago."

Robb wiped his brow. "So? So what? So we'd steal a few pieces of junk from some dead Indians. Sell the crap to a rich patsy. No one got hurt."

"No one got hurt until Morty got sick."

"Asshole called the Feds."

"We know."

"He ratted us out," Robb shouted. "He ruined everything. Why didn't he go off someplace and die?"

"Turn yourself in," Forrest said in a soft, trust-me, I-could-help tone. "Explain about the accident. Please. You don't want to kill us."

Robb hesitated, then blew out a breath and shook his head, his expression almost sad. "No. It's too late. Smith…"

Forrest let out a groan. "You killed him, too?"

Rob's mouth worked, like he wanted to say something, but then he tossed me the necklace. "Let's get this done."

I caught it.

"Do your hocus-pocus and open the damn cave."

The necklace warmed in my hands, much hotter than body temperature. The cat radiated heat.

*Power.*

I gulped in air and placed it over my shoulders. The drums beat so loudly, I couldn't think. I fisted my hands to keep them from trembling and stood in front of the cave entrance. I waited, not sure what to do next.

# CHAPTER 26

"Hold up the cat," Forrest whispered.

I stared at her for a moment, confused.

"Put the necklace up in the light." Her tone grew more insistent. She tipped her head to one side. "HE told me."

I raised one eyebrow, and then held the pendant over my head with both hands. Rays of light from the rising sun reflected off the cat's eyes and suddenly the entrance to the cave appeared in the back of the cliff wall.

Drums pounded from inside the cave.

Robb gave a shout and raced toward the opening, climbing over the boulders piled by the entrance.

The drums echoed louder, and I covered my ears. I doubled over in pain and dropped to my knees. After Robb disappeared inside the dark entrance, Forrest knelt beside me.

Then the drums stopped.

Quiet. Only a single eagle called from above.

I rested my hands on the sand and waited, dragging in air to clear my mind. Forrest helped me to my feet. We followed Robb, but stopped near the opening.

The Magician stood at the back of the dimly lit cave. Shadows hid his face.

Forrest drew in a quick breath. "Do you see him?"

"Yes."

"Me too."

Robb knelt over the sacred bones, staring at the treasure. "Incredible," he shouted. He licked his lips and picked up the decorated staff, then the sacred pot painted with an eagle. He gathered artifacts into his arms, reaching across the scatter of bones for more. "The stuff's worth millions."

The Magician moved forward and stood in the center of the small cave. A purple-white light rippled over the ceiling, but Robb didn't notice.

Forrest took a step closer, but I pulled her back. The cliff wall in front of us became solid again.

Robb's faint screams seeped through the rock.

\*\*\*\*

"Do you think he's a believer yet?" Manny shouted from above us.

I glanced up, surprised. "Tempting to leave him there to find out," I called, and then chuckled.

Manny slid down the rope and landed with a thud and a puff of dust. "Yeah, but then we'd have to explain another body."

"What will the ghost do to him?" Forrest asked.

"Don't know," I said. "The big problem is, I don't know if I can open the cave again."

"No need." Manny pulled out his revolver and walked straight through the rock. Eventually Robb's screams stopped.

Epilogue

*The following week.*

I handed Forrest a bowl of chili and scooted in next to her. She grinned at me, and my heart did a double thump.

"This chili's terrific, George." Manny shoveled another overflowing spoonful into his mouth.

"Thanks." George brought the pan from the stove to the table and ladled more of the spicy meal into Angel Wing's bowl, then passed around a basket of the freshly made tortillas. "The kids did most of the work."

"We make a pretty good team," Forrest said, nudging me with her shoulder.

Rocky and Gina appeared at the side door of the Trading Post. "Sorry we're late." They pulled up chairs, and George filled their bowls.

"How'd the hearing go?" I asked.

Rocky scooted in Gina's chair. "Robb will stand trial for murder."

"Probably three counts, unless they can find Zalo," Gina added. "Your testimony about what happened that morning on the cliff made the judge furious. He threatened to add two counts of kidnapping and attempted murder to the charges."

I gave a low whistle.

Rocky grinned. "Robb will be in jail for the rest of

his life."

I put down my spoon and rubbed my brow. "I don't understand how we all missed what the sheriff was up to."

George shrugged and patted me on the shoulder.

"He used to be a good guy," I continued.

"People make mistakes. Robb didn't start off a murderer." George pulled up a rickety chair and joined the circle. "He got caught up in something he couldn't control. Fear of being discovered made him do things he never would have even considered a few years ago."

Forrest squeezed my hand, and I glanced around the table at my family's faces. My heart warmed, and not from the peppers in the chili. My family. Finally. I cared…no, loved them. They cared for me. Protected me. Loved me.

There was one big question I still needed to ask, and this was the time. "Manny, who are you?"

Everyone stopped mid-chew and waited in silence. I glanced at George, but my guardian only shrugged.

Manny set his tortilla on the side of his bowl and rubbed his ear for a moment. Then he smiled. "You've heard the old story of the apprentice who stole the grave relics from the Magician."

"He was killed." I said. "Fell off a cliff. That was why I needed to return the artifacts to the Magician's grave when I was twelve. They gave the Magician back his power to protect the people."

"Well this time, the Magician was wise enough to train a better man. A second apprentice."

Forrest's eyes got big. "Are you a ghost?"

Manny chuckled and put up a hand. "No. I'm very much alive. Born and raised on the Hopi reservation.

I'm that ancient apprentice's too-many-greats-to-count grandson. Since the Magician recovered his power three years ago, I have served him. Protected him and our people. I was already a federal agent working on the reservation, but now I have...let's just say, a bigger job."

"Then why does he need me?" I asked.

Manny's dark eyes turned fierce. "We all need you." He rose and paced the room for a moment before returning to stand at the head of the table.

I swallowed, my heart banging in my chest like the valves of Forrest's junk jeep.

Manny leveled his gaze at me. "The Magician was a great man. The most powerful leader of his time. But that time is long past, and he knows this. The tribes need a living man to lead them. You are his direct blood. You were chosen before you were born."

"Wow," Forrest whispered. "Told you this was important."

"Did my mother know? My father?"

"Yes. When you were a young child, your mother taught you the ancient language."

"She told me the stories."

"Your father would have continued your training as you grew."

"He was killed in the war before my mother was murdered." My lungs squeezed tighter, and I fought for air.

Manny waited a few ticks of the clock on the wall.

Finally, I could listen again.

"George was then charged with your early training, and you will continue to live with him for several more years. In this modern time, your education must be twofold. You must not only master our People's knowledge and customs, but also those of the wider world. Only then can you lead us. Protect us. Maybe even protect the world."

"But you said you're Hopi. Josh's also Yavapai," Forrest broke in.

"Our people share blood and tradition. Many Hopi left the valley and moved north to join the people of the mesas a thousand years ago," I explained. "The Yavapai continued to live in the valley. They joined with other tribes who migrated here."

Manny nodded. "We are of one ancient blood. One ancient tradition." He drew up his chair. "The artifacts you will need for the future are safe. The necklace and the flute are yours to learn from and use. George and I will teach you."

"There will be other items you must search for and discover," George added. "You will need patience." His voice sounded grave, but I trusted the light in his eyes.

I turned to Forrest and tipped up her chin until she met my gaze. "Will you help me?"

Her smile widened and her blue eyes sparkled. "Yes."

"I always knew!" Angel Wings grinned at me. "Forrest is part of your destiny."

Coyote and the Bird Girls
From Hopi Coyote Tales Istutuwutsi
Ekkehart Molotki and Michael Lomatuway'ma
(A few small punctuation changes, for clarity.)

Aliksa'i. They say, long ago people were settled at Sikyatki. Lots of birds were also living there, among them the Bird Girls, who were always busy grinding corn. One day, as they were grinding, Coyote Girl chanced upon them. She inquired. "What are you doing?"

The Bird Girls answered that they were grinding corn.

"You're really doing that very nicely. I would like to grind with you."

The Birds consented because they were afraid of Coyote. "All right, you can join us, but first go pick some juniper berries. When you have picked some, bring them here, and then you too can have your turn at grinding."

"Agreed," Coyote cried and trotted off in search of the berries.

Meanwhile, the Bird Girls were discussing the matter among themselves. They were still a little frightened of Coyote.

"She won't harm you," the older Birds said reassuringly.

It wasn't long before Coyote Girl returned with a big load of juniper berries. The Birds cleared a spot for her so that she, too, could grind. It was incredible. Although somewhat awkwardly, Coyote Girl was grinding away alongside the Birds. While they were doing their work, the birds were also singing. Coyote Girl was all ears. The Bird Girls had cute voices. The song that they were singing went like this:

Bird Girl, Bird Girl,
Brush the cornmeal off the grinding stone.
Bird Girl, Bird Girl,
Brush the cornmeal off the grinding stone.
Callus, callus are the nails.
Callus, callus are the horns.
Meehe'e'e hew, hew, hew.

When they had finished the song, the Birds flew up into the air. They flew around for a while, and then settled down again by their grinding stones. They got back in line and continued with their grinding work. Coyote watched with fascination and then said, "I'd very much like to sing like you while I grind. Once I've learned the song, I could also fly like you."

Some of the Bird Girls replied, "Don't worry. You're bound to learn the song."

And so, indeed, while the Birds were grinding, Coyote Girl listened with great concentration. Some portions of the song she had already mastered. In the meantime, the Birds had soared up into the air several more times, and each time they resumed grinding, Coyote Girl chanted along with them. Her voice was very loud and scared the Birds. This is how she started the song.

Bird Girl, Bird Girl,
Brush the cornmeal off the grinding stone.

Only this much had she learned of the song so far, and then she couldn't sing on anymore. The Birds were chirping cutely. And sure enough, when they had finished, they soared up into the air anew. After winging around for a while, they again descended. In this fashion, Coyote Girl eventually learned the song by heart. She sang along very nicely with the Birds now. Once again, when they had finished, all the Birds were airborne, and only Coyote Girl was left behind on the ground.

This time, when the Birds flew back down, she turned to them and asked, "Couldn't you share your wing feathers with me? Then I could take off and fly like you."

The Birds agreed without hesitation, and said they would fit her with feathers. Presently they began to stick their plumes into Coyote wherever she needed to be feathered. They even attached a tail on her. With those plumes, she would be able to glide about with the Birds. Coyote Girl gazed in wonderment at herself. "Now I look almost like you. I will probably fly as well as you," she exclaimed.

Some of the Bird Girls were still scared. They feared Coyote. But then they lined up at their grinding stones again and began grinding once more. Coyote Girl ground along with them, and while they were working the Bird Girls chanted their little song. When the song had ended, they soared up, and Coyote Girl took wing with them. She didn't fly up very high, but hovered low above the ground. When the Birds sailed back to their grinding stones, Coyote did the same, landing by her metate. She looked at herself proudly and cried, "Wow, I made out just about like you: I actually flew up like you. I'm sure the next time I'll fly as high as you."

One of the Bird Girls—she was the oldest of the sisters—replied, "Yes, you'll probably do that just like us."

And so they ground once more. When their song

was finished, they flew up once again, and believe it or not, Coyote was flying around quite high this time. Some of the Birds, however, were still frightened of Coyote and said to their oldest sister, "We're still scared of her: She shouldn't be doing this here with us. She still might eat us."

"She can't harm us. Don't even think about that. You need not be afraid," their oldest sister calmed them down.

Back on the ground they all began grinding, as before. When they were through, they flew up again, and this time Coyote circled around like the Birds, extremely high. What a fantastic view she had from up there. "From here one can really see everything!" Coyote exclaimed.

"Of course," the Bird Girls shouted back. "Well, let's dive back down again."

Coyote Girl flew ahead and headed straight for her metate. Presently the oldest sister turned to some of the others and said, "We'll fly one more time. When we have Coyote all the way up here, we'll take all our feathers back. So fly way up into the sky this time. Then we'll rush up to her and pluck our feathers from her."

"All right, all right," everybody replied enthusiastically. With that the Birds fluttered back down to their metates. Coyote Girl was extremely proud of herself. "Well, now I can really fly like you. I'll have to find myself some wings somewhere," she said.

Once more they started grinding, and as they were singing, Coyote Girl sang along in her deep, deep voice. She thundered along so low that she frightened the

Birds. Feathered as she was, she presented quite a sight. When the song came to an end, they all soared up to the sky. This time the Birds flew way, way up. When they reached a point high up in the sky, the oldest sister gave the signal. "Now!" she shouted to her younger sisters.

Immediately the Birds all pressed up to Coyote Girl. She was still enjoying her flight and marveling at the view when the Birds rushed up to her and fell to plucking out their feathers. "This must be my feather! This must be mine! This one here belongs to me!" With shouts like these, they tore out all their feathers from Coyote.

Poor Coyote Girl was featherless now and plummeted from that height. She hit the ground and was killed instantly. Apparently she struck the top of a rock and died on the spot. There Coyote Girl was now lying.

"Well, we need no longer be afraid of that critter. She probably would have eaten us: that's why she carried on with us like that," the Bird Girls agreed. And so the Bird Girls, there at Sikyatki, brought Coyote Girl to her death. And here the story ends.

## A word about the author...

Along with teaching, Joy began her writing career by publishing children's historical fiction. She later found writing romantic suspense fulfilled her need for travel and romance. Joy grew up in Arizona and always felt a special affinity for the haunts of the central part of the state. She lives with her husband and two dogs near Silicon Valley and the mythical town of Sereno. http://www.ejbrighton.com

Thank you for purchasing
this publication of The Wild Rose Press, Inc.

For questions or more information
contact us at
info@thewildrosepress.com.

The Wild Rose Press, Inc.
www.thewildrosepress.com